JAMES O. WEEKS

NODDING'S
PEOPLE

Cover: Rebekah Wetmore
Editor: Andrew Wetmore

ISBN: 978-1-990187-71-1
First edition May, 2023

MOOSE HOUSE
PUBLICATIONS

2475 Perotte Road
Annapolis County, NS
B0S 1A0

moosehousepress.com
info@moosehousepress.com

We live and work in Mi'kma'ki, the ancestral and unceded territory of the Mi'kmaw people. This territory is covered by the "Treaties of Peace and Friendship" which Mi'kmaw and Wolastoqiyik (Maliseet) people first signed with the British Crown in 1725. The treaties did not deal with surrender of lands and resources but in fact recognized Mi'kmaq and Wolastoqiyik (Maliseet) title and established the rules for what was to be an ongoing relationship between nations. We are all Treaty people.

To Anne,
whose love and support
have made my life complete.

Nodding's People

James O. Weeks

1: Worse by the minute

Driving down the hill outside Truro, Nodding glanced up into his rearview mirror and saw a set of headlights coming much too quickly. His eyes shifted back to the road in time to see brake lights ahead and one car sliding into the passing lane. It was time to get off the highway.

"Good," he said aloud. Just beyond the icy patch was an exit. He could get off there, drink some coffee, and wait for a salt truck to come along. It had been sleeting for half an hour, but this was the first sign of ice on the highway.

"Easy now," he said to the truck's headlights, getting closer now. He had slowed to twenty himself, moving steadily along the shiny road.

The truck kept coming. Then the cab's wheels passed him, spraying his windshield, and Nodding glanced over at the trailer as the rear of his Forester caved in.

He was flung back against the seat, and glass nuggets bounced against the dash and onto his lap. The Subaru veered left and slid across the passing lane into the grass median, where the brakes finally caught, and he stopped.

"Crap."

He looked around to see what had hit him. The truck was stopping on the shoulder across from him, and only when he peered at it did he see the second trailer, jack-knifed and sliding sideways along the road.

He felt cold air and climbed out to see what had happened to his car.

The truck had hit the Subaru squarely in the back, above the bumper. The spare tire was intact, but the door holding it had been driven in, the window broken. Both rear lights were smashed, but the car looked as though he could drive it home.

"Hey, buddy!"

He looked over at the truck across the highway. The driver was leaning out of his window.

"Try to get your car over here on the shoulder before someone else slides into it. This whole stretch is solid ice."

"Right," he said.

He slipped once, then held onto the side of the car until he reached the door and climbed in. Even the grass was slippery where the day's light snow now had a covering of ice.

There were no other cars in sight, so he pulled across the highway and followed the truck a few hundred feet toward the exit, where the shoulder was much wider. He pulled up behind the second trailer, a Scotia freighter, its bright green and yellow letters glimmering with sleet in his headlights, and climbed out again.

"You okay?" The driver hurried back from his cab, glancing into the car. "You alone?"

"Yeah," Nodding said, feeling the cold. "I'm fine."

He looked up at the driver, who was at least six three and solid. He had short, curly hair and was wearing pressed jeans and a denim jacket. "I think I can drive the car. The back is just shoved in."

"Thank God no one was hurt. I can't even see a scratch on my rig," the driver said. "This road is getting worse by the minute."

He scuffed a boot on the ice and looked up the hill at distant headlights. "How's about we walk up on the shoulder a bit further, just in case?"

He led the way around the Subaru's front, so they could talk in the Forester's headlights.

"Now what's that?" the driver said, looking up. The lights made them squint, but they heard the squeal of scraping metal, then a loud crash, just beyond the Forester. Then they saw the yellow salt truck, huge even on its side, sliding by in the roadway no more than twenty feet from them. It moved on past the truck, finally coming to rest in the middle of the road.

Nodding took a step toward the wreck, but the driver grabbed his arm.

"No. I don't want you anywhere out on that road. If you get hurt, the company will fry my butt. Let me check it out."

He went down the highway in little steps, while Nodding backed further onto the shoulder. He thought about flares and looked at his car. They were somewhere in the back, probably pinned under part of the door. He gave up and looked up the highway.

Another salt truck was inching down the grade, its yellow warning lights shimmering in the wetness and reflecting off the roadway ice. It braked and finally stopped in the road to protect the overturned truck.

"That guy yonder is one lucky pilgrim," the driver said, hurrying back to him. "When I got there he was standing up in his cab, talking on his radio. So I helped him climb out and now his partner's here."

"Lucky he wasn't killed," Nodding said. He felt detached from everything, as though he were in a slow-motion movie.

"This hill is still a mess, and it's gonna be hours before it's cleared off," the driver said. "What say we get off here and go over to that truck stop across the way? At least we can be safe and dry."

"Fine with me," Nodding said. "We can call the RCMP from over there."

"My name is Tobias," the driver said. "Call me Toby." He held out a huge, icy hand.

"Dave Nodding." He took the hand and shook it.

"Dave," Toby dropped his hand. "Would you join me in a moment of prayer?"

"Here?" Nodding said, looking at Tobias, who had folded his hands and closed his eyes. "Why not?" He bowed his head.

"Lord of the Trans Canada Highway, we thank thee for saving us from being hurt or even squashed dead here on the highway. Please lend thy strength to the road crews this evening, so that no other pilgrims are injured in this weather." Toby paused for a moment and Nodding coughed. "Amen."

"Amen," Nodding said quietly. He wondered what would happen next.

"Let's get inside," Toby said.

He made his way to his cab and climbed in, then drove slowly to straighten the trailers, while Nodding got into his car. They crept down the exit ramp and under the highway to the bright lights of the truck stop.

Toby pulled his double trailer into a parking slot next to a number of other trucks, while Nodding pulled his Subaru into the car lot next to the restaurant.

"You lock it up?" Toby said, walking carefully across the lot to him. "These fellas can fall to temptation sometimes." He held the restaurant door open. "But God loves us all."

Inside the door was a huge truck tire, lying on a dummy in a suit, wearing a Trudeau mask. "TIRED OF THIS GUY!" was written on the tire. Next to the tire was a sign that read "NO MORE TRUCK WITH PRESCRIPTION COSTS!"

Toby stopped and examined the display. "It used to be the Nova Scotia premier. All they do is change the mask."

He dug in his pocket for his wallet and took out a card. "Let me call the dispatcher first. Then we can trade names and all that stuff." He found a row of quiet chairs where he could make his call.

Nodding had never been in a truck stop like this one, a restaurant and store that catered to professional drivers. While Toby was on the phone Nodding watched another driver buying a radio at the counter.

"My old one just conked out, and on a night like this," he said, smiling at Nodding. "I'd be dipped in shit without one, I can tell you that."

"Dave?" Toby had his hand over his phone's mouthpiece. "Dispatcher says I gotta wait here, to meet an adjuster. If you can hang around awhile, he can cut papers and save you time in getting your repairs paid for."

"Sure," Nodding said. "I'm not in any hurry to get back on those roads."

Toby spoke to the dispatcher and then hung up. "Let me get you a cup of coffee," he said. "It's gonna be awhile."

He led the way into the restaurant, where they sat in a booth and ordered from a blonde who was at least sixty and wore a starched white uniform like nurses used to wear when Nodding was a boy.

"Oh, come on, honey," she said to Toby. "Don't you want no pie tonight?" She winked at Nodding. "The preacher here likes his desserts. It's about the only excitement he has anymore."

"Oh heck," Toby said. "Bring me a piece of the apple. But no ice cream this time. I'm putting on pounds, Lena."

"How about you, honey?"

"Just coffee for now," Nodding said.

For a moment they sat uneasily, staring at each other. Nodding felt a little out of place in his dress overcoat and tie.

"You a salesman?" Toby asked.

The coffee arrived, and they took a moment to stir in sugar and to sip it. Toby seemed to fit in perfectly in his jeans, sweatshirt, and denim jacket. Nodding watched him pull the jacket off and fold it carefully before putting it on the seat beside him.

"I run the food service at St. Benedict's in Antigonish."

"You the boss, or do you actually cook?"

"A little of both," he said. "Mostly, I work with ordering the food and planning menus. But every few days I work the grill or put together a recipe."

"That's a fine university," Toby said. "I know some of the students from church, when they're home." He frowned as his pie arrived with ice cream, but dug in anyway. "What brings you down this way?"

"I was in Dartmouth for a wedding," Nodding said. "I figured I could beat the bad weather, but I didn't make it."

"Golly, I'm sorry. You know these double rigs go wherever they want, once they start sliding. I was lucky my cab stayed straight, or I could have really made a mess out there."

"It didn't seem icy until that hill."

"They don't touch that part of the road," Toby said. "The 102 is famous for its greasy spots. I was here three years ago when a friend of mine slid off the road in the underpass. He took a little sports car with him; killed the driver right out. My buddy lost his license and he's still not driving." He shook his head and forked another bite of apple pie into his mouth.

"Damned if it ain't the Preacher!"

Standing in the doorway behind Nodding was a trucker with a mouth missing several teeth and a long, scruffy beard. He was about six feet tall but weighed well over two hundred. He had on dirty jeans and a tee shirt that said HAGAN'S HAVEN. In one hand he held a greasy winter parka. He walked over to the professional driver section and sat at the counter, swinging on his stool to face their table.

"What's new, Hagan?" Toby asked. He turned his head to talk

over his shoulder at the counter.

"Not a damned thing, except this damned ice. I got a schedule to keep."

Nodding noticed rings of dark skin on each arm just below the elbow and realized it was dirt. He wondered what could have caused it.

"Lena," Hagan called. "Can't you move any faster? No wonder your husbands keep leaving you."

"I threw the last one out," she said, taking her time getting to the counter. "The old geezer was almost as obnoxious as you are, Hagan. I could take his mouth, but once he started leaving his teeth around the house, I'd had enough. He never even brushed the gross things."

She took out her pad. "Want me to read you the menu? We're fresh out of colouring books."

"Nothing on it worth reading," he said. "Give me a double order of mashed potatoes and an order of stuffing with gravy. Coffee to drink."

"A little something to hold body and soul together?" Toby said.

"Gotta keep my energy up, a night like this." Hagan looked over at Nodding, "Who's this, some kind of missionary?"

"No," Nodding said. "I run a cafeteria and do some cooking."

"Then you don't want to be in here, man," Hagan said.

"Shut your mouth, Hagan," Lena called from the kitchen door. "For someone who always gripes, you spend a lot of time at that counter."

She carried a plate over and put it down in front of him. "You sure you don't want some bread with this?"

"Nah," he said. "No flavour in that there Styrofoam."

"Hagan and I used to drive for the same freight line," Toby said, "if you can believe it."

"Still might if it wasn't for that little pissant of a dispatcher,"

13

Hagan said, his mouth full. "Now he's gone, maybe I ought to come back."

"This dispatcher we had was an unhappy man," Toby said.

"A Goddamn pissant, Preacher"

"Anyway, one day Hagan gave him a whole box of fancy chocolates, and the fella couldn't believe it."

"Told him it was to sweeten him up," Hagan explained. "Only they wasn't real candy. I gave the real ones to the wife. Then I put chocolate laxatives in wrappers, and that damned fool ate every one. Never offered to share a one. Just ate them all. He was in the shitter for two days, and I got fired."

"Things haven't been the same without you," Toby said. "A lot quieter."

"You oughta come west and drive for Melchior," Hagan said. "We keep things hoppin'."

"No way," Toby said. He smiled at Nodding. "Those guys haul some wild cargo, explosives and all. That's not for me. I want a load that just sits there."

"You hear about our load down in the Valley last week? Whole trailer got stole right out of a truck stop, in plain sight. Damn if it isn't enough to blow up a town."

"I'm hauling motorcycle parts," Toby said. "That's just fine with me."

"You boys ready for more coffee?" Lena said, holding up her pot. "Don't think you should have any," she said to Hagan. "Your wife wants you to fall asleep as soon as you get home."

"Won't be getting there tonight," he said. "But I will take another order of stuffing."

"Want another cup?" Toby said. "That adjuster won't get here for awhile."

"Sure," Nodding said, pulling off his coat.

"Heard you mention an adjuster?" Hagan said.

"Yeah, I bumped this fella's car out on the hill," Toby said.

"There's a salt truck laying out there now."

"It almost hit us," Nodding said. "It slid right by."

"Damn," Hagan said. "Here I hoped you was coming to improve the food in this place. You live in Truro?"

"No. Outside Antigonish."

"Not too wild," Hagan said. "Lots of kids and priests. Now, Truro has some excitement."

"This one's on me," Toby said, draining his cup and taking the check up to the counter. "See you out front, Hagan."

Nodding drained his mug, then followed Toby out to the entrance. A few drivers were standing around, looking out at the weather.

2: Right out of that steeple

"Let's sit over by the pinball machine," Toby said. "We can watch the door from there."

They walked over and settled into two of the uncomfortable plastic chairs. Toby sat in one with a built-in ashtray. "This chair's an antique," he said. "You smoke?"

"No," Nodding said. "Never have."

"I used to," Toby said. "Now I give my cigarette and beer money to the church. Not as much fun, but it does more good."

He folded his hands across his stomach and leaned back, the chair creaking. "You got a wife or anyone else you should call? I hate to hold you up this way."

"No, I live by myself. Not even a dog to feed."

"When I married my wife she already had two daughters. But they won't expect me until morning, anyhow."

"Must have been a change, getting a wife and family all at once."

"It surely was, but it was what I needed, Dave. Now there's something to look forward to when I come home."

Toby looked over at him. "You brought up around Dartmouth? You said you were at a wedding."

"I used to live there," Nodding said. "I was a chef at a restaurant down by the harbour. I was there two years, but things changed and I needed to move on."

"I've felt that way myself," Toby said. "You go to a friend's wedding?"

"My old girlfriend's. We were planning to get engaged, but she said she wasn't quite ready yet. The next thing I knew, she had moved in with her old boyfriend. I told her it was over and left town."

He shook his head and looked at his feet. He hadn't talked about this to anyone, and he wondered why he was telling it to this strange truck driver.

"Must have been a tough trial," Toby said. "But God does test his children."

He leaned over and touched Nodding's arm lightly. "What church you do you go to, Dave? Your pastor could help you get through this."

"I was brought up Anglican," he said. "But I haven't really found a church in Antigonish I like."

"We go to the Gospel Tabernacle of Light," Toby said. "I've taken to helping out with the services when the preacher needs me. I like driving and all, but when the holy work calls, I have to answer."

"I guess so."

"That's why they call me the Preacher."

Toby leaned back again and crossed his legs. He was wearing cowboy boots with small white crosses etched into the leather. "For a good many years I was a wild pup. Heck, I used to wake up in bed with someone I didn't remember, and then leave to find out I was in a town I didn't recognize. Yes sir." He nodded at Nodding's expression. "I was one of Satan's sinners and worked at it regular."

"What made you change?"

"I was down the states, in Ohio, on a long run and I was coming through the town I am named for. Right on the Ohio River, a little place called Belpre."

"That's your name?"

"Yes, sir, Belpre William Tobias, but the kids all called me Billy. My parents were originally from there, but lived up in Cape Breton.

My father worked as a miner for years. But anyway, I was driving through and the next thing I know I'm in a church parking lot, throwing up in the middle of the night, when the bell begins to ring. You know, Dave, the Holy Spirit came right out of that steeple, along with the pigeons, and it filled my soul. I was saved, and I darn near cried the whole way home."

"Your life must have changed a lot since then."

"My life is full," Toby said. "The very week after I started going to church, I met Jean. She was divorced because her husband had been a drunk and smoked drugs. Carried on right in front of the kids. Next thing you know we started courting and decided to get married. Ever since then life has been wonderful."

"I'm glad it all worked out," Nodding said.

"That's the thing, Dave. It didn't just work out. I came home to the Lord and he set me back on the highway in style. The company got me a new tractor, and I have one of those plastic Jesus statues standing up there on the dashboard to remind me of my blessings."

He leaned forward. "You don't think they're too Catholic or nothing, do you?"

"No, not at all." Nodding glanced over at the door, but no one was coming in.

"Good," Toby said, leaning back again. "I kinda like it." He smiled and nodded, then looked at Nodding. "It must have been a real trial to your spirit, losing your girl."

"It was rough," Nodding said. "I was ready to get married there for awhile, but I guess I barely knew her. It was a real shock. So I moved away, and we talked every night. I thought maybe she'd change her mind once I left, but she never did."

"She have a nice wedding? In a church and all?"

"Oh, yeah. All our old friends were there. I knew going would be awkward, but I couldn't stay away. You know?"

"You say her name was Rachel?"

18

"She was named after her grandmother," Nodding said.

"You know her name comes from the Bible originally," Toby said. "Rachel was married to Jacob and had one heck of a time having any kids until the Lord took pity on her. I mean this is after years of trying and old Jacob even got another wife and had babies with her in the meantime. Rachel had some kind of awful row with her father, too, as I recall."

He shrugged. "I haven't learned my Old Testament as well as I should, yet. There's just so much good news about Jesus that I get caught up in the Gospels."

"I didn't know where her name came from."

"Well, I'll pray for you both, Dave. For her wedded state and for your state of mind. It takes a lot of strength to pull away like you did. I doubt if I could have done it."

"I don't know," Nodding said. "I didn't really do much. It all just happened. Maybe I just ran away from it all by moving."

"Well, let me ask you. Do you have a girlfriend in Antigonish?"

"No," he said. "I work, go to the store, and go home. I've gone to faculty parties, but I end up supervising the food. It's been pretty dull."

"Then you didn't run away," Toby said. "If I was you, I'd get myself to a few good church socials. Meet some girls who won't go running off on you, and when the right one comes along, settle down. Marriage is a wonderful institution, and you seem like a good man."

They looked up at a young man coming through the door with a briefcase.

3: A flickering reflection

"Lord help him," Toby said. "This looks like an insurance fella."

The man saw them and came over. His face was bright pink, and he was wearing icy half-moon glasses. "I slipped out there and split the seat right out of my new pants," he said, looking at Toby. "I'm from Provincial Adjusters. Did someone here call in a crash?"

"You got us first try," Toby said. "I'm Tobias. I drive for Scotia."

"Rich Valentine, here."

"Appreciate you coming out, Rich. This is Dave Nodding."

"Hi Dave," Valentine said. "You must be from the dispatcher's office."

"No, I'm the guy he hit," Nodding said.

"Oh," Valentine said. "That makes it all a lot easier. Brother, what a night, eh? At least no one was hurt or killed. I really hate crashes like that. They're depressing."

"The Lord was watching over us tonight," Toby said.

"Whatever," Valentine said. "I decided when I started this job it could get pretty gruesome, so I take my mind off it by writing poetry. What kind of car do you drive?" He smiled at Nodding over his glasses. "I'll give you a little demonstration."

"Subaru Forester."

"Very safe car," Valentine said. "Now give it a listen."

He closed his eyes for a moment, then opened them and smiled.

Slid on the ice,

then hit by a truck.
Poor little Forester
feels out of luck.

He clapped his gloved hands once and nodded. "It's like a haiku, a short poem full of sensory images but limited in syllables. It's an Asian form, and I thought it would be appropriate for a Subaru."

"I was never too good with poetry," Toby said. "But I do like to recite hymns. Sometimes I even sing, out on the road."

"Really." Valentine glanced at him. "Well. Let's take down all of the information, and then I'll want some pictures of the car and truck." He took a chair next to them. "Have you called the police?"

"Not yet," Nodding said. "Should we?"

"Not unless you want to," Valentine said. "Let's start with you telling me what happened."

Nodding carefully went through the chain of events, while Valentine wrote everything down.

"You guys were lucky," he said to Toby. "As slippery as it is out there tonight, you managed to end up alright."

"Luck didn't have a part," Toby said.

"That so?" Valentine looked up over his glasses.

"It was our Lord and Saviour Jesus Christ on the roads," Toby said. "Keeping us pilgrims safe on our journeys." He looked at Valentine. "Aren't you going to write down what I say, too?"

"Right," Valentine said. He began to scribble while Toby repeated his version, which matched Nodding's.

"I think we all agree," Valentine said. "I don't think the police will be needed. I'll take some pictures and inspect your car, Mr. Nodding. When you get home, get an estimate from a body shop and call me. We'll take care of everything."

He took out his mobile. "Let's check out the weather."

Toby and Nodding pulled on their coats and followed Valentine towards the door.

"Yo!" Hagan stood in the restaurant entrance, an ice cream cone in his hand. "Get the preacher to bless that car of yours, buddy. You'll need it on them roads tonight."

"Of all the desserts that tonight I'd deem," Toby said, "most unusual would be ice cream."

Valentine smiled. "I like that one. I rarely venture beyond accident report verse. It's a specialized field."

"This is Mr. Valentine from the adjuster's office," Toby said.

"Oh," Hagan said. "Well, if you need a character witness or anything , these two guys is solid as shit. My name is Hagan, if you want to write it down. Chester Festus Hagan."

"I bet your parents liked Gunsmoke," Valentine said.

"No shit, Sherlock. They oughta take you off these cases and put you on murders. Truth be told, I got planted right on the trailer floor during the show. My old man wouldn't even turn off the tv to go to the bedroom. I half believe he thought that character was real. In fact, I got a poem made up about it, too."

"Do you write too?" Valentine said.

"Not lessen I have to," Hagan said. "Now listen:

> Roses are red,
> violets are purple.
> I got my start
> in a GUNSMOKE commercial.

"That's not bad," Toby said.

"It could use some polish," Valentine said.

"I'll tell you what you can polish, buddy," Hagan said, pushing the rest of his ice cream cone into his mouth.

One potato, two potato, three potato, four.

You can shove this poetry shit right out the door.

He laughed and waved at Nodding, who was buttoning his coat. "Time for us all to hit the road."

"Safe trip," Nodding said. "Nice talking with you."

"Hey, same here," Hagan said. "It's nice to meet another educated fella from time to time, except for old halo breath here."

"Thanks," Nodding said, stepping out into the sleet, which seemed to be easing up. He led Valentine over to his car; then stood back while the man checked the damage carefully, taking pictures from every side.

Finally the adjuster was finished, and he handed his card to Nodding. "Call me tomorrow," he said. "And drive carefully tonight."

"I think I'll stop at a motel," Nodding said. "It still looks icy."

"Thanks for being so patient, Dave," Toby said as they shook hands. "I'll be praying for you and Rachel. May Jesus guide your Subaru along the highway tonight. Amen."

He squeezed Nodding's hand, then led Valentine over to his truck, which appeared undamaged.

Nodding climbed into his car and started it, then sat back until the warmth melted the ice on his window. It had been such a long day, with so many emotions.

The wedding had almost been a relief, after all these months. He had been happy to see the many friendly faces, all urging him to come back. But it had been time to leave, to break away.

He smiled now: his new life was waiting, though really it was still as empty as it had been when he had first moved. He liked his employees, but they all went home to friends and families after dinner cleanup. His neighbours were cheerful, but beyond a hello or two he barely knew them.

Nodding knew he was quiet and not aggressive, and he enjoyed his privacy, too. But lately, sitting in front of his television, he had begun to wonder if his privacy was turning into loneliness.

The windows were clearing. He glanced at his watch. It was almost one.

He backed up slowly, the tires sliding a bit on the parking lot glaze. He crawled out of the parking lot and headed for the 104.

The ramp had been salted. The highway truck was still on its side, but policemen were directing traffic around it, so Nodding pulled onto the highway and drove west. The sleet had stopped, but it was getting colder.

For the first fifteen minutes he was fine, but then the day began to take its toll. His feet were cold, his neck and shoulders sore, and his hands were beginning to tremble.

Ahead to the right, he saw a sign for the Paradise Lodge, and he slowed for the exit ramp. He coasted the Subaru into the parking lot, then carefully made his way into the lobby.

"Welcome to Paradise," he heard as he came into the lobby. A smiling girl stood behind the counter. She was young, probably a college student, and beautiful. Her eyes were gray and looked too deep for such a pretty face. "The roads look pretty nasty out there."

"They are," he said. "Do you happen to have a room for the night?"

"Of course," she said, putting a registration form on the counter. She handed him the credit card machine, and he swiped it before filling out the form. He wrote down his plate number and handed her the form.

"You're from Antigonish?" she said, looking at the form. "My friend works at a steak place there. She said it's a real bargain, especially on the weekends."

She handed him a plastic key card. "This will give you access to the executive elevator and open your room. Just go down that hall, and the elevator is on your left at the end."

"Thanks," he said. He realized he had no idea what his room

would be costing. And with that thought came the realization that he didn't care.

"The pool and exercise centre are open all night," she said.

Nodding thanked her again and made his way back out to the Subaru. He climbed into the back seat and retrieved his suitcase, brushing glass nuggets onto the floor. Once again he crossed the parking lot, almost falling once, then felt the welcome warmth of the lobby as he opened the door.

"Have a pleasant night, Mr. Nodding," the girl said.

He found the elevator, pushed the button, then slid his card into the special slot. Tonight he didn't feel the least bit like an executive.

His room was familiar and warm. He put in a wake-up request by punching in a code on the room telephone, then got undressed and took a hot shower. He was too tired to watch television, so he turned off the lamp and climbed into bed.

It wasn't working. He was tired, so worn out he felt like crying, but the truck-stop coffee kept his mind working and energy pumping in weak jolts through his system.

Images came and went, of Toby, of the salt truck, of Rachel in her wedding dress. And the road came back. He felt the bounces and swaying as though he were still driving, even when he finally opened his eyes and looked at the ceiling. It was lit with a flickering reflection, which meant the rain must be melting the ice. But he knew it was getting colder outside, if anything.

He tried to close his eyes again, but it was no use. For a moment he lay staring at the window, then finally rolled off the bed and walked over to it. He fumbled for a moment at the curtain, then found the cord and pulled it.

He looked down, not on the parking lot, but on a large indoor swimming pool. His window was really a sliding door that opened onto a small balcony overlooking the pool, a steaming whirlpool bath, and an empty courtyard bordered by plants and small trees.

Nodding reached for the handle and was about to open the door when he saw movement and stopped. The girl from the front desk was walking across the courtyard below him in a robe, moving slowly. She reached the whirlpool and took off her robe, folding it carefully and draping it over a chair. She was wearing a bright blue, two piece bathing suit.

Nodding watched her reach down and flick a switch, turning on the whirlpool, then step slowly into it and sink into the white, swirling foam. She looked up at his room but he felt detached and simply stared back. Behind her, the ripples from the swimming pool sparkled in the light, and he stared at their flashes, feeling his energy finally fade. He looked back at the whirlpool.

The girl was still staring up at the balconies. As though satisfied no one was awake and watching, she reached behind her, then lifted the blue top to her suit out of the foam and dropped it beside the whirlpool.

Nodding stared quietly at the foam but felt nothing. He turned and moved back to the bed.

4: I don't understand bumpers

When the telephone rang to wake him, Nodding answered it quickly, then lay back on his bed. He glanced around the room as though seeing it for the first time, and realized the window curtains were still drawn. He climbed out of bed and looked down at the pool below. The dream, if it had been one, seemed to fit into the night's events somehow, so he left it all alone and took a morning shower.

After breakfast, Nodding checked out of the hotel, pleased that his bill was reasonable, and joined about a dozen guests in the sanded parking lot. The weather was clear and cold. As he moved carefully toward the Subaru, he smiled at the variety of ice-scraping techniques others were using, ranging from pounding on the ice with their fists to picking at it with the ferrule of an umbrella.

Nodding picked up his scraper, moved to the front of the car, and gave the scraper a firm push across the icy window. The blade immediately broke off from the wooden handle, leaving him with a small plastic strip. Nodding stared at the windshield, then got into the car, started the engine, and waited for the defroster to do the job.

The drive home was slow at first, but gradually, as the road improved after Truro, cars began moving at a reasonable pace. It didn't really matter, of course, because he had taken an extra day of vacation in case he was tired. But eventually he pulled into Tranquility, the new townhome development where he lived, and that was growing by leaps and bounds.

Somehow just seeing his front door made last night's accident distant, less frightening. He pulled into his parking space, climbed out, and went back to inspect the damage in daylight. Seeing the crushed metal, he felt lucky to be unhurt.

"Gracious, David, what happened?"

He looked up and smiled at Mrs. Saks, his neighbour from across the parking lot. Neighbours joked that she spent her days gathering news, and she was on the job this morning.

"I got hit by a truck down near Truro," he said.

"Not one of those with the loud horn and giant tires?" She clucked her tongue at his nod. "You're lucky to be alive. How badly are you hurt?"

"I'm fine," he said. "The car held up. I guess I'm lucky."

"I should say so," she said. "You never know with these modern cars. I wouldn't have one, myself. I want something solid around me. That's why I've kept the old Buick all these years. I feel so safe in it, don't you know?"

"Sure," he said with a smile. "I guess I'd better get in and unpack. I have to find a body shop and get this taken care of."

"Speaking of feeling safe, I don't know how long I can keep living here in Antigonish," she said, stepping closer. "This used to be such a quiet place."

"What do you mean?"

She said, lowered her voice. "I'm getting pretty suspicious about some goings-on around here. We could be in a war anytime, don't you know, and that Mr. Mayoubi might do just about anything. He's a come-from-away and you never know. He could be dangerous."

"Wissam is from Egypt," Nodding said, looking over at his neighbour's townhouse. "I don't think he's involved much with North Korea or even Syria."

"You never know. If he has ties overseas anything could happen."

"Really, I wouldn't worry. Wissam's worked for the telephone company for five years. He doesn't seem too concerned with politics."

"I hope you're right," Mrs. Saks said, looking doubtful. Her real name was Sakalouckas, but she hardly used it anymore. "Most of my name died with my husband," she would say. "Besides, this way people think I own that New York department store."

"I better get home and change the wash," she said, grabbing Nodding's sleeve. "I'm glad you're safe."

"Thanks, Mrs. Saks."

Nodding watched her cross the street, then picked up his suitcase and went up the steps to the townhouse door. He'd get his mail later, after he unpacked.

The house smelled clean, but a little stuffy. He had spent his last night at home cleaning, since nothing bothered him more than coming home to a mess.

There was one message on his phone, so he listened to it while he took off his coat and hung it up.

"Hi, David, this is Toby. I just got home this morning at nine thirty. I got stuck again and again and finally had to put on chains. Just wanted to thank you for waiting around for the adjuster and all. Listen, Dave, if the insurance don't come through right away, call me, and I'll see what I can do. Now, I meant it when I said I'd be praying for you. I'm just one man, but I'm trying to live the love that Jesus wanted. God bless you now, Dave. Bye."

Nodding saved the message, then looked up body shops on his phone. The first listing was simply called Auto Body Shop, and it was just across town.

He pulled a parka out of the closet and went back outside. He waved at Mrs. Saks in her window, climbed into the Subaru, and headed out.

The Auto Body Shop was in an old building behind the shopping centre where he bought his groceries. He parked the Subaru on the ramp and went inside to a small office area.

"Hello, there," a small man of about fifty said. He was standing in the doorway to the service area. "Can I help you?"

"My Subaru got hit by a truck," Nodding said. "I need an estimate for repairing the rear end."

"Not a problem," the man said, holding out his hand. "My name is Nick. How'd you find us back here?"

"I looked online. I'm Dave Nodding."

"A pleasure to meet you," Nick said. "I like to know my customers by name. Too many shops don't care about that, but not here."

He reached for a clipboard hanging on the wall and stuck a printed estimate form on it. "You gotta do more than fix fenders in this business. You gotta think, too. Like my listing online. My name is Venezia, Nicholas Venezia. But if I say 'Venezia's Body Shop', my listing shows off way down the list, right? Just saying 'Auto Body Shop' puts me right up at the top. And it worked, see? Here you are."

He looked around to a closed door that said GENTS and said, "Vincent, get the telephone if it rings."

No one answered, but Nick led Nodding out to inspect the Subaru.

"Holy," he said after a quick glance. "Look at this. Not a scratch on your bumper, but the rest gets smashed. What hit you, some kinda tank?"

"One of those double trailers."

"Oh, yeah. Then you're lucky it hit back here and not up front. A rear door is a lot easier to replace than an engine, you know?"

He made some notes on his clipboard and then knelt down and looked under the car. "She held up pretty good. Let's go back in the warm now."

Inside the shop Nick waved Nodding to a kitchen chair next to an old, cluttered desk. Pulling a large parts catalog out of the bottom drawer, he began jotting down prices next to his notes.

Nodding looked around at the small office, which was badly in need of cleaning. Besides the door to the repair area, another led to the lone bathroom.

"Any calls, Vincent?"

"No," a voice said from behind the bathroom door. "Hey, when you call out for those subs, ask for a large coffee, too. It's chilly in here."

"Instead of the diet soda?"

"Yeah. It's too cold for that."

"Vincent used to work out here at the desk," Nick said, dropping the catalog back in the drawer and shoving it closed. He started punching numbers on an old adding machine. "But we talked all the time. Now, that don't bother me, but Vincent does the bills and keeps the books, and he started making mistakes, on account of being distracted. So now he goes into the can when he works. Says it gives him privacy so he can concentrate."

"I swear it works," Vincent said from behind the door. "I don't get bothered here. Some days I don't even come out."

"This is Dave Nodding, Vince." Nick tore off the paper from the adding machine and began to copy figures onto the estimate form. "He got hit by a truck. Slid over the bumper and didn't leave a mark until the hatchback door."

"Nice to meet you," Vincent said. "I don't understand bumpers these days. Half the time you miss them when you hit something. Nick will tell you. It's just something with all these wrecked cars. It's scary to see how they get hit. I don't even drive my car any more, right, Nick?"

"He's right," Nick said, handing Nodding the estimate sheet. "Comes in at about six thousand dollars. Yeah, I pick up Vince every morning and drive him in. Says he's afraid he'd mess up a

31

new car if he ever bought one. Now, this here is with all new parts. If the insurance guy gives you any trouble, I can lower it with some used pieces. But I think you're okay here."

"I'll call the guy today and see what he says."

"You make sure he pays for a rental car," Nick said. "This may take a week or so, what with painting. You need a rental."

"I can tell you a couple of places to call," Vincent said from behind the door. "Tip-Top has an office a block from here. Dumb name, but their cars are reliable and clean. So give me a call when you hear."

"Vince usually answers the phone when I can't," Nick said. "We had a wall phone installed in there for him. Keeps distractions down."

"Yeah, but it's getting pretty crowded," Vincent said. "The computer isn't bad, but I keep knocking the phone when I use the printer."

"I'll give you a call tomorrow," Nodding said.

He shook hands with Nick, nodded at the bathroom door, and went back out to his car.

5: Zombie

It was almost three, but Nodding decided to stop by his office for a few minutes. He turned up the heat in the Subaru and drove across town.

Because the food service took regular deliveries, Nodding's office was close to the alley and the loading dock. He parked and went into the cafeteria, where he saw Kwasi Davis, in his white server's uniform, sitting at a table with a coffee mug.

"Hey Dave, welcome back," he said. "Man, I told you not to go. You look like you just got home from your own funeral. You shoulda stayed away from there."

"Well, it's over."

"It was over when you moved out here," Kwasi said. "Rule number four in my book says 'Once you leave, don't look back.' You not only looked, you went back and stepped in it."

"I know," Nodding said. "How are things going?"

"Smooth and quiet. The ice threw off our early deliveries, but everything's in by now. Austi had to call in because her daughter had her baby, so I'm doubling on the line."

"Good," Nodding said.

The room was almost empty, but soon it would fill up with the dinner crowd. Most of the students would come through the line, but some had food in their rooms or got a snack from a vending machine.

Looking over at the machines, he saw two women digging in

their purses for loonies and gave them a wave. Audrey Katz had been in accounting for more than ten years and had been stopping by every week to share recipe suggestions. He'd tried some of her ideas (like throwing cheese cubes into the meatloaf) and had won her friendship and patronage at once. Jenny Porter was younger, skinny, and generally sullen.

"You look beat," Kwasi said. "Like a corpse."

"I feel that way," Nodding said.

Kwasi was an observant and energetic guy, working on a business degree. He was good with the students, great with the staff, but didn't have a clue about cooking. It wouldn't be long until he moved up and out of the food service. As Nodding stood to leave, he heard a thump from the vending machines.

"Mr. Nodding." Audrey was waving at him. Jenny was on her knees in front of a candy machine, her arms stuck in the delivery chute. "Hurry up."

"Are you all right?" Nodding hurried over with Kwasi. "What happened?"

"I'm stuck in your damned machine," Jenny said. "I wanted cookies but they didn't fall off the curlicue when I put in my money. It was just wedged so I figured I could reach it. But then I slipped and now I'm caught."

"I didn't think anyone could reach up there," Audrey said. "I told her to give it a good kick like normal, but then we saw you there. We probably should have asked for a refund."

"My wrist is double jointed or something," Jenny said. "I can always bend it this way. But I can't raise up high enough to see how I'm caught." She was bent over with her eyes level with the slot door.

"It looks like your ring is hooked on the wire holder," Kwasi said. "Does it hurt?"

"My hand doesn't hurt, but my back can't take much more of this bending over. I'm going to report this!"

"Calm down, Mrs. Porker," 'Kwasi said. "Maybe if you wiggle your hand, the ring will fall off."

"I don't want it to fall off," she said. "I promised Conrad I would never take it off, no matter how uncomfortable it got. That's why it got stuck, because it's about four sizes too big. And my name isn't Porker, and I'm not married."

"It belonged to Conrad's mother," Audrey said. "She was a large woman, as I hear it. Jenny has to wrap the ring with adhesive tape to make it fit."

"Do you mind waiting until I'm out of this thing to discuss my life? I'm stuck here."

"I'm sorry, Miss Porter," Kwasi said. "Could you try wiggling your finger a bit? Maybe the ring will slip off the wire."

"Give it a try, Jenny," Audrey said. "The boys will be coming in soon and here you'll be with your rump in the air."

"It's not like I planned it or anything," Jenny said. "And Conrad says my ass looks just perfect."

"I probably shouldn't say anything," Audrey said. She turned to Nodding. "Now, don't you men listen."

"We won't," Nodding said.

He and Kwasi turned away and stared at the kitchen.

"It's your underwear," Audrey said. "It's black and it shows right through your white pants. Even the lace shows." She turned to Nodding. "Can't you get her out?"

"What are you looking at?" Jenny said, twisting to look up at Nodding. "Don't you stare at me."

"I'm looking at the cookies," he said, peering into the machine and pulling coins from his pocket. He dropped the coins into the slot.

"Stop it. What are you doing?"

Jenny twisted her body away from the machine, brushing Kwasi.

"Oh! Watch your hands," she said.

"You bumped my leg," he said, stepping back. He was smiling. Audrey Katz looked over at him, trying to keep her mouth grim.

"Hold on," Nodding said, pushing a button on the machine.

"It's screwing," Jenny said. "Oh, my God."

"There," Nodding said. The machine had twisted enough to release her ring, and she pulled free, rubbing her elbow. "Are you okay?"

"No thanks to that machine," she said. "The administration will hear about this."

"I expect the whole place will hear about it," Audrey said. "I wish I'd thought to record it!"

"You're supposed to be my friend," Jenny said. "And you just sat here talking about my ass with these men."

"Here's your cookie," Kwasi said.

Jenny snatched it and stormed out.

"Nice to see you back," Audrey said. "But it looks like your vacation wore you out."

"I'm going home to sleep now," he said. He smiled at her as she left, and said to Kwasi out the side of his mouth, "Now, that doesn't happen every day."

"Sure beats discussing casserole recipes with Mrs. Katz."

"Did she come up with another one?"

"Gave me a choice of six. They're on your desk. Maybe we oughta try one. Put some flesh on our Miss Porter." He smiled and saluted as Nodding left.

Nodding drove down the road to his small development. He waved to Mrs. Saks, went inside, and realized he was hungry.

He turned on the radio and listened as he popped a chicken and noodle casserole into the microwave. Every weekend he cooked a bunch up and froze them for quick dinners when he wasn't at work.

The news came on, and it frightened him. There was always fighting about to break out somewhere. There were many steps toward peace being taken these days, and then somewhere else it all fell apart. It reminded him of the Clarence Darrow quote he had memorized in high school: 'History repeats itself. That's one of the things wrong with history.'

"What the hell," he said out loud. If he was really serious about doing anything, he'd have to get out of the kitchen and into politics, and that simply wasn't in the books. He hoped this latest tension would ease.

The microwave buzzer pulled him back to the present, and he took out his meal. He pulled off the cover, stirred the casserole, then spooned it onto a plate. He sprinkled a little paprika on it out of habit, then carried it over to his table. He came back for a beer, took a swallow from the can and went back to the table. He finally felt relaxed as he settled down to eat, back in a routine he enjoyed.

It had been a pretty weird day. He remembered the smell of paint in the auto body shop and was tempted to call to see if Vincent was still in the bathroom. He smiled.

And then he thought of Jenny Porter with her taped engagement ring and black underwear. "Mrs. Porker," he said, shaking his head.

That was no mistake. Kwasi made it his business to know his regular customers. It was just his way of getting in a dig, one he could smile at later. He was a strange guy, an angry guy underneath, Nodding guessed.

There had been a time or two when some student had made some racial joke and Nodding had seen Kwasi's eyes flash. But Kwasi was cool. He would never jeopardize his position with any customer by losing control. Nodding would always step in quickly and tell the student to keep his remarks decent.

Jenny Porter must have said something once that had bothered Kwasi, or maybe she had acted superior, and Kwasi had filed it away, and the jab was ready today when she was vulnerable. Kwasi had style.

Kwasi wasn't his real name. His parents had named him Angelo Davis, after activist Angela Davis. Kwasi said he had chosen his African name as soon as they told him he was named after a woman. He had kept it ever since, but lately had been talking about using Kevin as a professional name. He thought it might be more acceptable in upper corporate circles.

Nodding knew Kwasi had friends and parents in Halifax, a life to go home to. Nodding had his casseroles, television, and the CBC.

He finished his plate, took it over to the dishwasher and realized he indeed felt like a zombie. He turned off the lights on his way to the bedroom. It was only five-thirty, but he didn't wake up until his alarm went off the next morning.

He woke up feeling happy for the first time in months. He hummed in the shower, but sobered up a bit as he watched the news. He watched a bit every morning with coffee, but he ate his breakfast at work.

Checking the time on his cell, he grabbed the adjuster's card and the body shop estimate and went out to his car.

He got to his office early. Despite a healthy appetite, he took a few minutes to look over his messages. Nothing looked too interesting or important, so he went out into the cafeteria and got a plate of scrambled eggs and home fries.

He was finishing his second cup of coffee when Audrey Katz sat down at his table. She was wearing a heavy, red cloth coat and a red knitted toque with a white maple leaf on it.

"Thanks for being so nice yesterday," she said. "You could have yelled at Jenny for reaching into your machine and all."

"She didn't do any harm," he said. "I'm just glad she didn't hurt herself."

"Well, I'm sending her over to apologize today," Audrey said.

"That girl has it rough at home, but she had no call to act so uppity with you and Mr. Davis. That was just silliness."

"Don't worry about it. I hear you dropped off some recipes."

"I just want you to take a peek at them," she said. "Your tuna casserole is good on these cold days, but these add just a bit more spice. Did I tell you I mailed some off to a recipe contest last month?"

"Why don't you quit over in accounting and join us here?"

"Oh, bother," she said. "I'm so used to that computer that I'd feel lost anywhere else." Audrey blushed, though, and left with a smile on her face. The students would love having her in the cafeteria.

Nodding checked in the kitchen, then went into his office to catch up on paperwork. He let Kwasi handle bills, scheduling, and purchase orders, but the menu and food orders he handled himself. He'd scheduled this week before he left, but unless he called in orders for next week, he might run short.

When he felt like he needed a break, Nodding picked up his cell and called Rich Valentine in Truro. "I got out to a body shop yesterday and got an estimate," he said. "I'll fax it when I hang up."

"Thanks," Valentine said. "Did they tell you the labour hourly?"

"No. But their phone number is on the estimate. They didn't break it down into parts and labour."

"I'll call them," Valentine said. "I always want to say, 'Give me the fax, sir, only the fax.'"

"Yeah," Nodding said. "I'll use the fax number from your card."

"We put our number on the card. We make it easy, not too hard."

"The repair will take at least a week. The guys at the body shop said I should ask about a rental."

"No problem," Valentine said. "But avoid the big companies. They charge a fortune."

"Thanks," Nodding said. "I appreciate it."

"No problem. I always say 'Our adjusters never fail because your check is in the mail.'"

Nodding hung up and dialed Vincent's number. It was busy, so he looked up Tip-Top Auto Rental and called them. He gave his name and information to a man named Stan, who assured him they'd have a car delivered to whatever body shop he wished within two hours of being notified. He told them he was using a shop down the street from their office, and there was a pause.

"That the one with the guy in the toilet?"

"Vincent."

"Right. Good work there, but he's a little different." Stan assured him it was all set.

"Thanks," Nodding said.

As he hung up, he caught sight of Jenny Porter standing in the cafeteria.

6: She could be a police

"Hi," Nodding said. "How's your finger today?"

"It's fine," Jenny said, holding it out so he could see. The ring was certainly huge, but the diamond was small and seemed dwarfed.

"Listen," she said. "I just came over to say I'm sorry for all that yesterday. I really messed up, I guess."

"No problem," he said, and thought of Valentine. "Has Audrey been on your case this morning?"

"Yeah," she said and smiled a little. "But I had already decided to come and say I was sorry. I feel so embarrassed. I must have looked so stupid."

"No, you didn't. I came in once and found a guy with his whole arm wedged up in the soda machine. We had to call the soda company, and they wanted an ambulance standing by in case he got cut. The newspaper heard the dispatch and sent a photographer. Now *that* guy looked stupid."

"I believe it," she said. "Was that here?"

"No, back in Dartmouth."

"Audrey told me you were up there visiting friends." Jenny looked at her nails. "She said you were pretty lonely down here."

"It's a little different here." *Audrey must have shared a lot.*

"If you feel like talking some day, I'm a good listener." She smiled a little, then blushed. "I mean, like during break or something. Conrad wouldn't mind that."

"Well, sure."

He had been about to say no, but there was something in her eyes that made him wait. And he was also a little curious about Conrad. "How about during lunch or break tomorrow?"

"Okay." She smiled again. "See you later."

She turned and Nodding couldn't help noting her blue pants.

He spent the next couple of hours helping get lunch ready. Austi was back on the grill, and preparations were running smoothly. When the food was ready for the lunch rush, Kwasi called him back to the office for a phone call.

"David? This is Vincent, at Auto Body Shop."

"Right, Vincent. How are things going?"

"It's cold in here, you know? If I keep the door open, I can't get any work done. But I freeze if I close it. And I can't fit a heater in here. So what else is new, right? Listen, the insurance adjuster called and sent me some papers, so now we're ready. You want to bring it in on Friday?"

"The sooner the better," Nodding said. "I hope the cheque will get here in time."

"Yeah, I talked with that Valentine guy before he sent me the paperwork. He said a week was no problem, but he acted a little weird. He read me a poem about your car and the crash. You know, I meet a lot of guys in this business, but he's the first that ever read me a poem."

"I know what you mean. I've heard him recite several."

"Oh, good, then. As long as it's not just me. Okay, we'll see you Friday, David."

That evening Nodding pulled into his parking space just as Wissam Mayoubi was climbing out of his car.

"Oh, David. I was going to look for you later."

"How are things going, Wissam?"

"Since you ask, it is not too well for me. I thought that with many new immigrants from Syria, I would stop getting stares of people at work for being Egyptian. But they still call me 'Arab'. And people do not know their geography. I explain where I am from, and still people ask if Egypt is next to Haiti."

"I would hope that people would learn," Nodding said.

"Many do not care to learn. Many people are kind and friendly. But some are not. That is why I wished to speak with you, David. I want to ask about the lady across the street, the one with the white hair. All day she sits and watches. When I come in or out, I see her curtains move. Is she maybe some kind of government police?"

"No, I think she's just a lonely old lady."

"Arabs and Muslim people are watched in many countries because we speak and act differently. I watch it on the news, so I wonder if maybe she could be a police. But you think no?"

"Let me talk with her, Wissam. I don't know if it will help, but I'll try."

"Thank you, my friend," Mayoubi said, shaking Nodding's hand. "I have friends from home coming to visit later this week, staying for a few days. They might be afraid."

"I'll try to talk with her tomorrow."

"I just see your car, David. What happened? Did you get hit at your work?" Wissam put down his briefcase and peered at the back of the Subaru carefully.

"I got hit by a truck on the 102," Nodding said. "It goes into the shop Friday, and I'll have a rental for about a week."

"Where is it good to rent cars? If my friends rent them, I won't have to drive them everywhere."

"There's a place just about a mile from here. It's called Tip-Top, and it's not very expensive."

"Cheap is good," Mayoubi said. "Tip-Top is a silly name, I think, but I will call them and say you recommend them."

"And I will talk to Mrs. Saks tomorrow, Wissam."

"Thank you again," he said, picking up his briefcase and heading up the stairs to his front door.

Nodding glanced across at the townhouse curtains, but they were closed. Shrugging, he went over and knocked anyway.

"David."

He turned when he heard the whisper, but no one was there.

"I'm here. In the Buick."

He peered at the car and saw the backseat window was down. "The driver's door is unlocked."

"Mrs. Saks, come on." He reached over and opened the door, but no light went on.

"I undid the bulb in case they were looking for a target."

"What are you talking about?"

"All day long Mr. Mayoubi has been coming and going. He brought in six bags from the grocery store. No one man can eat that much, David. I've done my fair share of cooking, believe you me. He's getting ready to feed a team of hooligans."

"Now what makes you think that?" Nodding looked back at her in the dark car. "Wissam just told me some of his friends from home are coming to town for a few days. Believe me, he's just as scared of you as you are of him."

"That proves it," she said. "If he were innocent, he wouldn't pay me a minute's mind. He's up to no good, that one. Can't you tell just by watching him?"

"Look, Mrs. Saks, we have to talk about this tomorrow. In the meantime, you keep an eye on him, but do it from your house. He'll spot you for certain if you keep sneaking out here."

"You didn't see me," she said.

"It's dark out. You could barely see *me*, either. Now why not go inside? It's dinner time."

"They eat human flesh," she muttered. She rolled up the window, opened the door and stepped out of the Buick. Nodding took her elbow to steady her on the pavement. "I read that somewhere years back."

"Who? Egyptians?"

"No. You still haven't caught on, David. The terrorists, wherever they're from. I saw it on the television, too."

"Egyptians aren't any more interested in human flesh than we are," he said. "I bet a lot of them are vegetarians."

"Brother, do they have you brainwashed," she said, letting him help her up the steps to her front door. "I know the evil these people do. But I'll think about this Egypt business a little. Maybe I'm being overly suspicious, but I'll be armed and ready just in case."

"Don't get ready to start fighting," Nodding said. "You don't really have a gun, do you?"

"My husband bought it back in the sixties, just in case the Russians came ashore in Halifax. We used to go there every summer and rent a little apartment for a month. Of course, back then it was quiet in the neighbourhood. Nowadays the whole place is crazy with cruise ships and teenagers. I went back there to visit just before you moved here. Minnie Storck had a place, you know, and I stayed with her. There were hooligans out on the streets at night, just carrying on. I came home and said I didn't care to see people with pink hair doing what they do right out in the open. I can see that sort of thing on cable any night."

"What about the gun?"

"I keep it right inside," she said, opening her door and turning on the light. She led him to the living room and opened a small drawer on an end table next to her couch. Inside was a black, shiny, dangerous-looking Luger,

"Is it loaded?"

"Heavens no," she said. "I wasn't born yesterday. I don't own any bullets for it. That would be simply too dangerous."

"It looks like it's in good shape," he said, bending over to look at it. The gun looked as though it had been cleaned recently.

"I know how to break it down and polish it. But these days I use baby oil and tissues for the job. Yesterday, I rubbed a little lemon oil on the handle, just to make it smell nice."

"It's a beauty. But it's also scary, Mrs. Saks. I don't want you getting carried away with this Wissam business and waving it around at anyone."

"I don't intend to take it out of the drawer," she said. "But I'm going to keep my eyes peeled, just in case something comes up."

"Just remember he has company coming," Nodding said, heading back to the door. "So the strangers you might see are only guests."

"I'll keep a low profile. I don't want them to realize I'm on their trail."

She smiled as he went out the door. "Be careful, David."

"I will," he said.

He thought of the casserole in his kitchen, but veered back to his car. "The hell with it," he told the parking lot.

He climbed in, started the engine, and backed out. Before he could go further, Mrs. Saks blinked her porch light at him.

No, just pizza wouldn't do. Beer and pizza might help, but even then he wasn't sure.

7: The trap

Friday morning was cloudy, but it felt warmer. Nodding left early to drop off his car.

No one was visible in the Auto Body Shop office when he went in, but he saw a light coming from under the bathroom door. "Good morning, Vincent," he said.

"That you, David? How are you this morning?"

"Fine. I'm just here to drop off the car. Is Nick around?"

"No, he went out for coffee and the bank. He took his wife out last night, so he's tired today."

"Can I just leave the keys on the counter?"

"I don't like getting a late start myself, so some nights I sleep over. I get some work done, and it's a change from home."

"I know what you mean," Nodding said, wondering if Vincent slept on the toilet. He put the keys on the counter. "I'll give you a call on Wednesday."

"I'll be here," Vincent said. "Your car will look brand new,"

Nodding went to the door, stopped himself from waving at the bathroom, and went out.

The Tip-Top office was a block away, a small room on the back of an office building. When Nodding opened the door, a young man in a short sleeve shirt stood up to greet him.

"You've reached the top," he said, reaching out to shake hands. "You must be Mr. Nodding."

"Right."

"Before we get started on the paperwork, I just want to say thank you," he said. "We rented five cars yesterday evening to the Mayoubi family on your referral."

"I'm glad you could help them out," Nodding. said. The office was awfully hot, and he noticed the young man was perspiring heavily, even this early.

"Well, business hasn't been booming," the young man said. "By the way, my name is Stan." They shook hands again. "At this rate, we'll put you on the payroll soon."

He let go of Nodding's hand and reached for a clipboard. "Now let's get you on the road."

Nodding got a small, white Hyundai and was on his way to work fifteen minutes later. The car was new, handled nicely, but smelled like cigar smoke. When he rolled down the window, the icy breeze felt like driving his own car with the back smashed in. But, by Wednesday, he'd have his own car back in good shape, so he turned up the heat and made it to work in time to prepare one of Audrey's recipes.

Jenny came in for an early lunch. Nodding watched her choose a table in a corner, so he got a cup of coffee and went over to join her. She had meatloaf and fruit salad and was frowning at her tray.

"Something wrong?" he asked.

"This meatloaf looks pretty weird," she said. "Audrey told me it had carrots and mushrooms in it, but I'm not so sure."

"It tastes good," he said. "I tried it to be sure." He sat down at the table. "Did she tell you to talk to me?"

"No," she said. "I don't do everything she tells me to do. She just mentioned you were kinda down, and since I'm a good listener, I figured I should be friendly. You were nice to me the other day, so I'm being friendly back."

"I appreciate it," he said. He glanced at her hands and saw she chewed her nails to the quick. "But I'm really okay."

"Good. So let's just talk, then. You like hanging out with these food guys?" She glanced over at Mabel on the serving line, who was sixty, solid, and missing some teeth.

"Not really," he said. "I get along with them all, and I've gotten to know Kwasi pretty well, but none of them are really friends."

"Him." She poked her meatloaf with her fork. "He tried hitting on me at the Christmas party with Conrad right over at the bar. If I'd told on him, Conrad would have whopped him right there, so I didn't. Who does he think he is?"

"He probably had a few drinks and was just being friendly."

"Conrad doesn't like black people." She finally took a bit of the meatloaf on her fork, tasted it, and put the fork back down.

"It wasn't Conrad he was interested in."

"Well, it was Conrad who would have been mad. I cut the guy off pretty fast."

"Don't like the meatloaf?" Nodding finished his coffee.

"I like the fruit better. We have lots of burgers and stuff at home. Conrad doesn't like fruit too much."

"You guys going to get married?"

"In a while, I guess," she said, looking down at her fruit. "Conrad says there's no hurry, and he gets mad when I ask about it."

"Been together long?"

"Four years. I was still in high school in Cape Breton when we started going out. Then Conrad got laid off, and he moved down here. My parents didn't seem to care what I did, so I came too."

"What's he do now?"

"Oh, he works maintenance over at the shopping centre. We live in a mobile about fifteen minutes out of town." Jenny finished the fruit and pushed the tray away. "We live pretty near the new supermarket, and Conrad had a job there, only he got in a fist fight with his supervisor."

"End of that job," Nodding said.

"No kidding. But she was a tough lady. Gave him a black eye."

"He fought a lady?"

"Don't matter to Conrad," she said. "He can get pretty mean when he's angry."

Jenny looked at Nodding, then glanced down. "Now, look. We ain't hardly talked at all about you, and lunch is almost over."

"That's okay. We can always do this again.".

"Sorry I talked on so much," she said. "I guess it makes me a little nervous. If Conrad knew I was eating alone with a guy, he'd crap. But you're a guy too, so you know how that is."

"Not everyone gets that jealous," Nodding said.

"Audrey said you were different than Conrad. She said your girl started dating some other guy, and you didn't care?"

"Not exactly. I cared,"

"Is that why you moved out here?"

"Rachel and I were seeing each other for over a year. We even talked about getting married. But then she asked how I'd feel if she went out once or twice with a guy from work."

"You *let* her?"

"I didn't like it, but I didn't own her. I told her to choose between the two of us, and she said she liked us both. It got to the point where I just had to leave town."

"Conrad would have put me in the hospital and killed the other guy. I can't believe you just let it happen."

"If she really loved me, she wouldn't have gone out with him," Nodding said.

"So she married him?"

"No. They got engaged, but then she fell in love with a shoe salesman. That's who she married."

"Maybe letting her go wasn't so crazy after all," Jenny said.

"I don't know. After I moved here, I just felt numb. First we were in love, then just I was in love, and now it's all over for good."

"Did you try to stop her?"

"It's all for the best," he said, smiling. "Now I've gone and used up the rest of your lunch break."

"You could have made her stay, though," Jenny said. "You could have gone after the guy and scared him off. That's what Conrad would do."

"You can't make someone love you," Nodding said. "Besides, that shoe salesman would have come along later."

"Conrad says women are naturally weak and can be tempted," she said, lowering her voice a bit. "He read about it in the newspaper. It's because our pelvis isn't straight or something. So it's up to the man to control the relationship. Like I said, if he knew I was having lunch with you, he'd at least twist my arms a bit. And that's just for having lunch."

"You mean he'd actually hurt you?" Nodding leaned forward in his chair.

"He does it all the time, if I don't behave," she said. "Not everyone thinks like you do."

She saw his expression. "It's not that bad, really. He's careful not to give me bruises where they would show and stuff. He's just a little over-protective and a bit physical. But when he's in a good mood it's kind of fun."

She smiled and leaned forward. "Like last week I had a couple of beers one night, and then he pulls out these handcuffs."

"You expect me to sit over there and starve, girl?" Audrey Katz brought her tray up to the table. She put it down and Nodding noticed she had chosen a tuna sandwich.

"No meatloaf?"

"I'm sorry," Jenny said, jumping up. "We just got talking."

"I had meatloaf for dinner last night," Audrey said, glancing at Jenny.

"I'll head over right now," Jenny said, picking up her tray.

"Thanks for talking," he said. "How about Monday?"

"Sure, I guess so," she said. "I'm going back over, Audrey."

"Conrad sounds like a real piece of work," Nodding said, watching Jenny cross the room.

"He's a dirty piece of sewage," Audrey said. "I was hoping she'd tell you about him, David. That girl needs help, but I don't know what else I can do. I tell her every day to leave him, but she won't. Poor child is only twenty."

"Well, I'll talk to her again Monday."

"You'd make a nice couple."

"That's not what I meant," he said. He waved across the room as Jenny went out the door. "It's just nice to talk to someone who isn't as pushy as you are." He smiled at Audrey's cackle as he went back to the office.

"You're falling into the trap, man," Kwasi said. "Old Audrey has you drooling at the bait, and you don't even know it's happening."

"I'm not trapped if I see it and avoid it. The girl needs a friend, that's all."

"Keep telling yourself that, man. You won't even feel it when the trap gets sprung. But you better cover your ass against that boyfriend of hers. He is one sick pup."

"Conrad? That's what Audrey says."

"For once in her life, she's right. Buddy of mine is a bank teller, down at the shopping centre branch. He says Conrad is one bad dude. He even beat up his woman supervisor for firing him."

"I thought that was what got him fired."

"No way. Word is, he saw a couple of girls shoplifting. He said he'll turn them over to the cops, and they got all hysterical. So Conrad takes them to the office to calm down and says he'll cut them a break. What he didn't know was the supervisor's car had a flat, so she came back to the office to call for a ride. She comes in, and there are the girls dancing naked as jaybirds for Conrad. He told them it was dance or cops. *That*'s what got him fired."

"He didn't tell Jenny that part."

"No surprise. And you better not either, man. Just forget it and stay healthy."

"Don't worry."

"I warned you once and now I'll shut up. It's one trap or another, the way I see it. It's just that sometimes you can't see it coming."

"Do you have a trap?"

"I got a couple," Kwasi said. "First, there's the colour trap. If I go home and act like I do here, my friends say I'm like an Oreo and give me all kinds of shit. If I act like I would at home when I'm here, I'd get all kinds of comments about my attitude. That's the work trap. I'm in the middle trap, because I don't know which to fall into. So I'm stuck. Then there's the name trap. No matter what I decide to call myself, one of the traps gets worse. But see, now I know those traps are there. Miss Jenny there doesn't see hers. All she knows is she isn't happy. And old Audrey Katz is in the lonely widow trap. She thinks giving out her recipes and advice will make her happy."

"So I'm getting close to the Conrad trap."

"And it's a dangerous one, man. But you're safe now, since you're in your own trap. You're in there hiding, and you've turned your trap into a cage. You're safe in there, or at least you were until you noticed the bait today."

"It isn't much of a cage if I can come out," Nodding said.

"We can all come out, that's the thing. But we don't, see?" He smiled and shook his head. "Once I figure that one out, I'll write a book and explain my Trap and Cage philosophy."

"I'll buy a copy."

"Don't hold your breath." Kwasi said with a smile.

8: A combination of boyfriend and father

After work Nodding got into his little white car and drove home. He parked, glanced over to see if Mrs. Saks was home, then noticed her Buick was gone. He smiled at the little line of white Hyundais like his in front of Mayoubi's house. Tip-Top must have bought in quantity.

He went inside and spent the evening watching television, only occasionally thinking about Jenny.

Saturday was a bright, crisp day, and Nodding decided to take an early walk around the neighbourhood. He walked along his street for about six blocks, then turned back.

Mrs. Saks was standing outside in a long coat, waiting for him. "They took off bright and early this morning," she said, nodding at the empty parking spaces in front of Mayoubi's house. "But I think the government is onto them now."

"Why?" Nodding said.

"There was a blue car here when I got up. It was parked a little down the street with its engine running. The driver looked like an undercover agent. I think his name is Elliot."

"Did you talk to him?" Nodding said, stepping closer.

"At that hour? Don't be silly, David. I wasn't even dressed. He just looks like an Elliot. But he drove away pretty soon after they did."

"Maybe he was here to pick someone up?"

"He left alone," she said. "It makes this whole case more mysterious."

"Did you get his license?"

"I didn't even think to try." she said, grabbing his arm. "I think I have some binoculars in the spare bureau. I'll go clean them up right away quick. Thanks, David."

She turned, then stopped. "Why are you driving a car like the spies? Who is this Tip-Top person on the stickers?"

"It's a rental company," Nodding said. "I told Wissam where I was renting a car so he got some for his guests. That's all."

"Good," she said. "I was beginning to worry they had brainwashed you. But try not to park right next to them or Elliot will get confused."

Nodding waved as she walked home, but realized it wasn't such a bad idea. He didn't know who the man in the blue car was, but in the dark his own car would be hard to find if parked with the others. He went inside, changed, and drove to work.

The college was quiet, but students had to eat, so Nodding kept the cafeteria open and serving. His weekend crew was small but experienced, mostly older workers wanting a little extra income. He spent a couple of hours in his office, until he finally finished all the paperwork he had missed while away.

He was about to turn off the computer and head for home, but then called up the college database. He entered his security code, then entered Jenny Porter's name. The screen told him she wasn't in the office at the moment. He turned off the desktop and headed for home.

He spent some time making an early dinner, French onion soup from a left-over stock, a small salad, and a chicken breast baked in a Marsala reduction, just as a change. *It would be fun to manage a restaurant someday*, he thought. At the university, everyone ate quickly, then went back to whatever was next on their schedule. In a restaurant, you were serving people who came by choice and who could linger over the meal.

He had thought about opening a kitchen in Cape Breton, but tonight was the first time since moving here that he had considered the old dream. But it would have to remain a dream until he saved a lot more money.

He finished his dinner with a cup of freshly-ground coffee.

Monday the world news woke Nodding to a gloomy day. Unless something happened to break the tension, American troops would be heading for the Middle East. He thought it was too late for an easy solution and headed out the door feeling tense.

"Good morning, David." Wissam was coming down his steps, briefcase in hand.

"Morning," Nodding said. "I had a chat with Mrs. Saks, but I don't know how much good it did."

"Thank you, I have explained to my visitors, in case they observe her. I believe I will send her some flowers and seek to be her friend."

"That would be very kind."

"Have you put new security in at your college?" Wissam asked. "The airports seem to have increased it quite a bit, even here, from what I saw on the news."

"Not that I can tell," Nodding said.

"At home we were used to such procedures, but here it is all upsetting. The company we use to ship telephone parts at work now uses trained dogs. It slows down our delivery times quite a bit."

"Our food deliveries seem to be as smooth as ever. The dogs would just get hungry if we had them."

"That is true," Wissan said with a laugh. "Oh well..." He waved and walked to his car, parked next to the string of white Hyundais.

Nodding climbed into his own and left, watching for the mysterious blue car, but without success.

Mrs. Saks called him at work just after eleven, sounding out of breath. "David, they knew I was watching, and they had him do it."

"Now calm down, Mrs. Saks. Tell me what happened."

"You're the only one I can trust. The RCMP officers don't care, and Elliot in the blue car just vanished."

"Please, just tell me what happened."

"That's what I'm doing, David, but you keep interrupting. Just sit tight and listen to me. Just after nine this morning a big truck drove in. It was this big tractor trailer and right away quick the terrorists scurried out and started carrying box after box after box of who knows what into Mayoubi's house. Pretty soon they finished, climbed into their little white cars, and off they went. And then it happened."

"What?"

"What I was telling you, David." She took a deep breath. "The big truck backed up and smooshed the front of my Buick. Then it drove off, nice as you please, so I couldn't follow them."

"Did the driver stop at all?"

"No, but he saw it. He jumped out and looked, then he got back in and off he went, before I could get down the steps. My fender is squeezed tight up against the tire. I would have gotten my gun but it was all the way inside."

"But you're sure he saw the damage?"

"That's what the Mountie asked, and I said I was positive. That driver was a foreign man, but he didn't look like the tourists. He just looked different." She sniffed. "I didn't tell the Mountie they were terrorists."

"That's probably good," Nodding said. "What did you say?"

"I said a big truck had delivered to Mr. Mayoubi and hit my car. I was too upset to remember anything about the truck, but I recalled you told me he worked at the phone company. So the Mountie called him at work."

"Then what?"

"He told them it was a private hauler and he would pay for the damage to my car. He sent over a tow truck and even sent me flowers."

"Good," Nodding said. "Do you feel better now?"

"He's a dickens," she said. "All smooth outside and pure evil inside. Believe you me, I checked over those flowers for a microphone or camera as soon as they came. I know he's up to no good. But now I'm stuck here, so now I need one of those little cars like you have."

"Call Tip-Top," he said and gave her the number. "They'll bring the car right to your house"

"I hope they have a car that isn't white," she said. "But I know the Mountie thinks I'm right."

"Why?"

"He was in disguise. Dressed all in dark, no red top or wide hat."

Nodding said goodbye and hung up. He thought about calling Mayoubi but decided the man's day was going badly enough.

"Trouble?" Kwasi said, leaning into the office.

"Just my neighbours going crazy. Somehow I'm trapped in the middle of it, too."

"Speaking of traps, there's one waiting for you out here."

Jenny had taken her tray to the same table they had shared Friday. She waved when he came out, and he smiled before getting his coffee and joining her.

"Have a nice weekend?" she said.

"It was quiet."

"Mine too."

"I thought about our conversation a few times," Nodding said.

"I did, too. I really haven't met anyone like you, who could just walk away without fighting to keep someone."

"I'm not sure she was ever mine to begin with. I hope she loved me, but I never felt like she belonged to me."

"I'm not putting it down. It's like, so gentle a way of thinking."

"I guess Conrad isn't always so gentle."

"He's never gentle," she said. "He never has been."

She took a bite of her cheeseburger, then said indistinctly, "There was one guy in high school who used to kind of like me, Greg. He played in the band and was in the academic classes with me, and I guess that made Conrad mad. Well, one day I stayed late after school to hear the band practice and then Greg gave me a ride home. That was it. He never kissed me or anything. But the next day Conrad blew up the car with Greg in it. He got burned and hurt just for being nice to me."

She paused to swallow. "No one could figure out what happened, but Conrad told me. That was the first time he ever hit me, that night."

"That's horrible," Nodding said, reaching across the table and taking her hand.

"He beat me so bad I couldn't walk for two days. He can be pretty mean."

"He must have a good side if you're still with him."

"He won't let me leave. Besides, he says he'd die if I left."

"Is there anything I can do?" Nodding said. He looked up and saw Kwasi watching him from across the room.

"You'd just get hurt and make it worse," she said. She wasn't eating now. "Here I started out to listen to you talk, and I've dumped all of my problems right in your lap. I'm sorry."

"You can get out of it."

"It's not that simple. I tried once, and it was so scary it was easier to go back. He plays these games, you know? He turns friends against you, and I don't think I can ever break away. If I went to anyone, he'd go after them."

"What about the police?"

"He'd find me," she said. 'I can't exactly go into hiding. Besides, it's not always like this. A lot of the time he's happy and it's fun."

"I wish there was some way I could help."

"You are helping," Jenny said. "I grew up with brothers and I was a tomboy until I was like thirteen, and I like being around guys. But usually if I start talking to a guy, he'll think I'm hitting on him. You haven't done that. It's nice just talking, you know?"

"You're wearing makeup," he said. He knew she looked a little different.

"Just a bit. Conrad lets me from time to time."

"I don't know how you stand it."

"But he takes care of me. That's the good side. When he and I started going out, I had parents who worked all day and didn't care what I did. Conrad did. He was like a combination of boyfriend and father. He's nice to me when I'm good and he punishes me when I'm bad."

"You're not a little kid anymore, Jenny," he said. *This isn't a trap*, he thought. *More like a whirlpool, and now I'm spinning faster*.

"I usually don't let it upset me," she said, her voice getting lower. "I don't even mind when he spanks me, you know. But last night he was drunk."

She looked up and he saw tears in her eyes. "Oh God, I'm so sorry. You haven't done anything but be a friend."

"You don't have anything to be sorry about."

She pulled her hand away and sat up. "No, wait." She took a big breath. "Last night he saw the clothes I had laid out for work. And they were a little different than the ones I usually wear. I just wanted to look a little nicer, for a change. And he was mad and he started to hurt me, and he made me say why I was dressing nicer. So you should be mad at me too, David, because he doesn't believe we just ate lunch together. He might come after you."

'Don't worry," Nodding said. "I'm more concerned about you than Conrad." He thought he sounded strong, but inside he felt small and cold.

"I have to stay away from you," she said. "I was going to eat lunch like nothing was wrong and then tell you. Because it was so nice on Friday. But I can't be near you anymore. He could walk in here at any minute. I'm so sorry."

She wiped her face with her napkin, met his eyes for a moment, then stood up and left the cafeteria.

"Great," he said.

He took her tray and his coffee cup back to the dish table, then took his mug and refilled it. Kwasi was checking the coffee.

"Snap, bang, pow," Nodding said. "Maybe we'll talk later."

"Cool," Kwasi said. He disappeared into the kitchen while Nodding went into the office and finalized a menu.

9: Get in line

When Nodding pulled into his street that evening, he saw no sign of a blue car. But instead of going home, he climbed the steps to see Mrs. Saks.

"Come in, David," she said. "Look out at the lot. They had a nice little black car for me and that young man Stanley said to say hello."

"Good. You know, I think you and Mr. Mayoubi need to get together and talk through this whole mess. It's getting ridiculous."

"It is not, David. You still don't understand," she said. "Now, I'll talk with him, because I want to see what he's like up close, but only if you're there to keep things under control."

"Good. I'll call him and see if he's free after dinner tonight. Let's take care of this before things get even more complicated."

"I agree," she said. "The sight of that truck hitting my Buick almost made me take a stroke right on the spot. Those huge letters on the side were bigger than my car by themselves."

"What did they say?" Nodding asked.

"MILKER," but this was no dairy truck. It was one of those big highway trucks."

"Did you tell the police?"

"I don't remember what I told them, I was so upset. But the police can't stop terrorists, David. We need more agents like Elliot on the case."

"I'll go call Wissam," he said.

"It's starting anytime."

"What is?"

"Their mission," she said. "Should we pick a secret password?"

"No! This has to stop."

He went down her steps and was in the street when Wissam drove in. He waited while the man got out of his car.

"It is a mess," Wissam said, shaking his head. "The police called me about the truck. Such a foolish driver."

"What happened? I only heard one side."

"That I can believe. One of my friends knows a man who owns a truck. They arranged to ship belongings of my family and friends here, until they are settled in. The man with the truck is not insured for such trips, I understand, so he drove away. He was wrong, and of course I shall pay for the repairs."

"This has upset Mrs. Saks. I hoped the two of you could talk this evening."

"Talking is good, David," Wissam said. "But tonight is not so good. I think she and I both need to calm down and tomorrow we will both feel better. I also have much work tonight."

"I'll talk with you tomorrow," Nodding said. "Thanks, Wissam."

Nodding watched his friend go inside, then went into his own house. He called Mrs. Saks, who agreed to a meeting on Tuesday evening. He pulled his curtains, shut out the intrigue, and made some dinner. Afterwards, he turned on the television and tried to forget the white slacks Jenny had been wearing again today.

Nodding looked out at the parking lot after his morning shower, and all was quiet. He dressed and left, meeting Wissam by their cars. It was a cold morning, and both of them had to scrape their windows. Luckily, Tip-Top had provided a good scraper with his rental.

"How about after dinner this evening?" Nodding said.

"I should be home by five," Wissam said. "I have kept the evening free."

"Good. She also thinks there's some spy in a blue car driving around here."

"A blue car?" Wissam looked around. "Perhaps it is a police?"

"I don't know."

"It always pays to be careful. I will look for a blue car as well."

They finished scraping and unlocked their cars. "See you tonight," Wissam said, closing his door.

Nodding followed him from the lot. There was no sign of life from Mrs. Saks.

When he got to his office, Nodding found a message to call Auto Body Shop. Nick answered on the first ring.

"Good news, David. The parts came in and your Forester is ready."

"Great," Nodding said, smiling at a bit of good news. "But my cheque isn't here yet, and I don't have that much money lying around."

"Tell you what," Nick said. "Give your insurance man a call and tell him the story. Let me know what he says, okay?"

"Fine. I'll call his office today."

"We'll be here. Our pipes froze last night and the shop is a mess. Lots of cleanup."

"Is Vincent okay?"

"Oh yeah, but he's mad," Nick said. "The bowl got cracked and his CD player got messed up. I guess all wet isn't good for electronics."

"I suppose not," Nodding said. "I'll call you back."

He hung up and called the insurance adjuster.

"You have reached Rich Valentine. All my customers are friends of mine."

"I hope so. This is David Nodding. I was wondering about my check for the Subaru."

"Right," Valentine said. "You were out on the ice, right? Let me check for you, uh, yup. Listen to this one, Dave:

> As true and regular as you suppose,
> you can depend on Scotia.
> If you slip and happen to wreck,
> it won't take long to get your cheque.

"Don't have mine yet, and my car is ready."

"Just a little poetic license, Dave. Your claim is in Moncton. They should process it in a week or so."

"Now, wait. You said the check would be mailed quickly."

"And it will be. I've done my part, Dave. You might be better off calling their office."

"Who do I ask for?"

"Just call the casualty department. I'll give them a jingle in a little while, so just sit back and try to smile."

"Thanks," Nodding said. He hung up without saying goodbye, just to make a point of being mad. Unless he knew who to ask for at the trucking office, he didn't think he'd accomplish much with a phone call.

Then he smiled, and found Toby's phone number on his phone. If nothing else, Toby had a supervisor, and he could work his way up the ladder that way. He punched in the number and sat back as Kwasi leaned in the door.

"Audrey Katz is here with some suggestions. You want me to take them?"

"No, I'll be out in a minute," he said. "No answer here anyway."

But before he got up, he dialed the terminal number, just to leave a message. He explained what he wanted to the operator, who told him to hang on.

"Jesus loves us all," a familiar voice said.

"Toby, this is David Nodding. I thought you'd be out on the road."

"Well, God bless you, Dave. I was just thinking of you. I'm stuck in the office today because my accident review is after lunch."

"Are you in any kind of trouble?"

"Heck no. It happens after every fender bender. It gives the managers a way to weed out the drivers they don't like, I guess. What can I do for you?"

"My cheque is lost somewhere in the system, and my car is ready. Could you find me a name to call in the casualty office?"

"I can do better. I got nothing to do this morning except drink bad coffee, so I'll ask around and see what I can find out. I'll call you back."

"Great," Nodding said. He gave him his office number, then thought of something. "By the way, is there a trucking company named Milker?"

"Almost," Toby said. "There's Melchior. Remember Hagan, the loud guy at the truck stop? He drives for them. Not too big a company. Why?"

"I'm not sure," Nodding said. "A guy driving a truck with something like that on the trailer hit my neighbour's car in our parking lot, then took off because he wasn't insured for private hauling."

"Sounds like something's messed up. I'll check the listings, but it's probably Melchior, and that don't ring true. They're strictly long distance haulers, and their drivers are insured up the wazoo, But I'll check it out, Dave. I was gonna give old Hagan a call. Heard his mother died unexpected the night we met him at the truck stop, so I wanted to let him know he was in my prayers,"

"That's too bad," Nodding said. "The truck thing is probably nothing, but I appreciate your help with the claim."

"God bless," Toby said. "I'll give you a holler soon."

Nodding went out into the cafeteria and saw Audrey Katz drinking an iced tea. He went over and sat down.

"So I hear you have more recipes?"

"I brought a couple down, but you still haven't finished my last batch," she said. "I'm worried, David. I started this whole mess with Jenny, and I'm sorry."

"You have nothing to be sorry for, Audrey."

"She's a mess today," she said, playing with her tea spoon. "She really thinks Conrad is going to come looking for you. She even gave him a wrong description of you. Said you were short and wore glasses."

"I haven't seen him yet. He'd have to get in line, anyhow. My car's in the shop and I can't get it out. The lady across the street is carrying an empty gun to scare my next door neighbour, who she thinks is a terrorist. And there may be an undercover cop driving around the street, watching us."

"I can't help thinking I started it all," Audrey said.

"You haven't caused any trouble," Nodding said, patting her shoulder.

"But was I right about you two? Do you like her?"

"Audrey," he said. "I have to get back to work."

"I don't think she'll come down today," Audrey said. "You'll have to come see her."

Nodding went into his office and called Mrs. Saks. She didn't answer.

He thought about going up to see Jenny, but decided to wait. Instead, he went into the kitchen to try one of Audrey's recipes for vegetable stew.

10: Not terrorists at all

It was a quiet day, so Nodding left early and drove down to Auto Body Shop. He hadn't heard from Toby, but wanted them to know he was working on the problem.

"David Nodding," Nick said. He was standing in the office. "How you coming?"

"I'm working on it, but I have to leave the car with you for a few more days."

"That's no problem. We got plenty to do here and plenty of room for your car, right?" He nodded at a man sitting at the desk, who nodded back. "David, you know Vincent, right?"

"Sure," Nodding said. Vincent was a younger version of Nick, short and solid. "Pipes getting fixed?"

"It's a mess," Vincent said, looking at the bathroom door. "It even smells like a shithouse now. Gonna get mildew, maybe black mould, mess up the whole room. Won't be the same, but I can't work out here, either."

"What choice we got, Vincent?" Nick said. "Maybe we could rig up a partition for you, like your own wall. It ain't like you'd be out in the shop and all."

"I hear you had a rough day, too," Vincent said, looking at Nodding.

"The insurance man is not my favourite right now," he said. "Could I ask a dumb question? Why not take that old bakery truck you have on blocks out back and make it into an office? It's a neat old truck. I was looking at it the other morning."

"The engine's no good," Nick said,

"You wouldn't have to drive it," Nodding said. "Paint it up, put some tires on it, and park it on the ramp. Or put it in the shop. If it's outside, it could be free advertising."

"You know, that might work," Vincent said. Looking up at Nick. "I could put in a desk, run in electric, and I'd have more room than in the hopper. We could even move over the file cabinet."

"Who could make it better than us, hey?"

"If it works, we could stick in a Chevy motor and I could drive it home. Something that big, I could feel safe again."

"Boy, you got a good idea here, David," Nick said. "We'd put a phone line in, just like before."

"Maybe a little cot, in case I wanted to sleep over," Vincent said. "But wait. Now I don't know."

"What?" Nick said.

"This chair ain't comfortable. I can't use a regular chair any more, Nick. I ain't used to them."

"So put in a toilet," Nodding said. "It doesn't have to be connected. It's your office: make it a place you'll be comfortable in."

"Yeah," Nick said. "What about it, Vincent? Wanna go out and check it over? Make some plans?"

"Come on out, David. Take a look with us." Vincent stood up and rubbed his hands together.

"I have to get going," Nodding said. "But when I come back for my car, I'll check it out. I promise."

"Hey, you get the credit if this works," Vincent said. "You know, Nicky, they won't run a cable to a truck, but what about a little satellite dish on the roof?"

They followed Nodding out the door walked around the building, throwing ideas back and forth, as he climbed into his rental.

On his way home, Nodding thought about the meeting with Mrs.

Saks and Wissam Mayoubi. It would ease the tension if it went well, but if it didn't, Wissam could get angry, too.

He pulled in at the supermarket and bought some crackers and cheese, then went next door and picked up a bottle of white wine. He already had soda and juice at home, if either chose to skip the wine.

When he got home, the little dark car was across the street, so he called and invited Mrs. Saks over at seven o'clock.

"Try to be nice," he said. "He's coming to make peace."

"I'll behave, David. But just you wait."

Wissam agreed to the evening time as well, so Nodding put the wine in to chill and heated up leftovers for dinner. He carried his plate to the living room and watched the news while he ate. Things had eased in Haiti, but new concerns about North Korea were being expressed.

Nodding cleared his plate, put the cheese and crackers out, and had just opened the wine when Mrs. Saks rang the bell.

"I know I'm fifteen minutes early," she said, letting him take her coat. "But I wanted to get here first and choose my seat. Where you sit is important in negotiations."

"Can I offer you a glass of wine?"

She sat in his armchair, leaving the couch vacant, then leaned over and peered at the cheese. "That sounds wonderful, dear," she said. "But only a wee bit. I want to keep my wits about me this evening."

He went to the kitchen, poured a glass, and brought it back with a leftover Christmas cocktail napkin. "The white one is cheddar, the soft one is brie, and there's some Dragon's Breath Blue as well."

"They look elegant, David. And these crackers are my favourite."

"I see on the news that things have settled down in Haiti," he said.

"Thank goodness," she said. "My friend Carla has a nephew

who's heading down there next month and she's been worried sick about him. I told her he should go to work at the post office and be safe at home, but you know young people." She took a sip of her wine. "Are you recording this meeting?"

"No," Nodding said. He glanced down at his phone, but no messages from Toby or Valentine had come through. "This is just to talk and see if we can work out a truce."

"The war hasn't even started yet, dear," she said, and then the doorbell rang.

Wissam hadn't bothered to put on a coat and was still in his white shirt, tie, and identification badge from the telephone company. "We were busy at work today," he said. "Please forgive me for being almost late."

"Would you care for a glass of wine or pop?" Nodding asked.

"A soda would be wonderful," Wissam said. He glanced at Mrs. Saks, who took a sip of her wine and kept her eyes on the cheese.

When Nodding brought him a glass of pop, he came over to the couch and sat down across from Mrs. Saks.

"Good evening to you," he said. "The weather seems to be warming up a bit."

"Spring isn't here quite yet," she said. "Mark my words, we're still in for some nasty winter weather."

"I want to thank you both for making time to meet this evening," Nodding said, sitting down next to Wissam. He noticed Mrs. Saks had moved the cheese over to her side of the coffee table. "There's been some, I guess, tension at our end of the street recently, so I think getting together to talk face to face should iron out any misunderstandings."

He looked at Mrs. Saks, who nodded, opened her mouth, and put a piece of cheddar on her tongue. She was still holding the cheese knife in her hand.

"I will be happy to start," Wissam said. "If I understand the problem, my guests seem suspicious to Mrs. Saks. The truck incident made the whole situation worse. But let me say that I not any kind of spy or evil agent for anyone. I have lived here in Canada for years. My homeland is Egypt, and we have been at peace with Canada for many years. I do not like North Korea, and neither do my guests. As Egyptians, our lives have been made harder by other mid-east countries, and so we come to your nation for freedom. My guests are simple businessmen like myself. One is my cousin Nassar, and the others are friends. I hope I can make you believe we are not spies, but I don't know how."

Mrs. Saks dabbed the corners of her mouth with the Christmas napkin and cleared her throat. She noticed the cheese knife in her other hand and put it back on the plate.

"My dear Mrs. Saks, is there anything I can tell you to help you understand?" Wissam said.

"I think I understand things pretty clearly," she said. "I have always been a suspicious person. Sometimes I'm glad that I am. I caught my brother stealing my allowance when I was a girl and, let me tell you, I got my revenge. We went down to the picture show on Saturday and when he asked for some of my cookies I gave him a dried out piece of soap. It only took a mouthful and he was up and running to the washroom. I told him the next day if he so much as looked at my piggy bank again I'd give him rat poison, and he straightened right up and behaved."

She shook her head a little ruefully. "But sometimes being suspicious makes life worse. I was always suspicious of my husband, but I doubt if he ever did anything wrong while he was alive. So maybe I've let the news on television stir me up. But whatever, now I don't think you are a terrorist, and I'm sorry I let my suspicions cloud my judgment."

"What made you change your mind?" Nodding said.

"I decided to find out for myself. When Mr. Mayoubi went out this morning, I followed him. He went straight to the telephone company. I even went up and asked at the information desk and they said he was in the sales department. They asked if I wanted to see him and I said no, but I went to the mall and watched him eat lunch with two other men, who were both Canadians, I assume."

She looked at Wissam. "It was a long day, and I haven't been so bored in years. You spent thirty minutes looking at computer magazines at the bookstore while I had to stand across the way in the arcade with some smelly teenagers who belonged in school. Anyway, I now know Mr. Mayoubi is no terrorist if he can stand a life like that."

She looked at Nodding and smiled. "May I have a little more wine, David?"

"Of course," Nodding said, taking her glass. "Another soda, Wissam?"

"No, thank you," Mayoubi said. "I did not think my day was that dull," he said. "I had a very pleasant lunch. But I suppose it wasn't very exciting."

He stood and reached across the coffee table for a cracker and cut a small wedge of brie. Mrs. Saks crossed her legs and watched him.

"I'm glad things can calm down now," Nodding said, coming back with the wine. "This went more smoothly than I thought it would."

"Like I said, now I see things clearly." Mrs. Saks took a sip of wine, put her glass on the coffee table, and looked at Nodding. "But I still don't know who that blue car belongs to. Everything else makes sense after tonight."

"I looked for that car myself," Mayoubi said. "It wasn't here when I came home this evening. It was all white cars and your black one at our dead end."

"Other cars were here earlier," Mrs. Saks said.

"But I didn't see the blue one." Nodding saw she was clenching the arms of the chair tightly.

"A big grey Lincoln did pull in before I got out of my car," she said to Mayoubi, who stared blankly back. "One of your guests got out of it before it drove away."

"They are arranging business deals," Mayoubi said. "It was probably a customer." He looked at Nodding and shrugged,

"My suspicions clouded my judgment," Mrs. Saks said, leaning forward. "But today it all came clear. You may really sell telephones, but there's something rotten going on with your guests."

"I sell computer equipment for commercial phone systems," Wissam said. "Not telephones."

"What are you saying, Mrs. Saks?"

"I was sitting in my car, not even trying to eavesdrop, when Mr. Mayoubi's friend climbed out of the car." She looked directly at Wissam. "I heard every word they said."

"What?" Mayoubi said, his face colouring. "What did they say?"

"Your friend said 'Thank you'," Mrs. Saks said.

Mayoubi sat back on the couch, staring at her. Mrs, Saks picked up her wine glass.

"Is that it?" Nodding asked.

"Of course not," she said, putting down the glass without drinking. "I'm not senile."

She looked at Mayoubi. "The man in the car said your guest was a drug dealer."

She looked at Nodding and nodded once. "So they aren't terrorists at all, but instead a band of heroin addicts."

"I must be losing my brain," Mayoubi said. "This is just not possible. My family is Muslim. My guests are as well. We do not drink alcohol, let alone use drugs. This is craziness,"

"Wait a minute," Nodding said. "Exactly what did you hear, Mrs Saks? Did the man in the car say Wissam's guest was a drug dealer? Were you close enough to be sure?"

"Not in those words," she said. "But I heard because he spoke very loudly. Mr. Mayoubi's guest said 'Thank you,' and the man in the car said, 'Next time, just stick to dealing in drugs.' I heard it clear as a bell."

"Wait," Wissam said, putting his hands on his head and closing his eyes. "Was my guest a short man, wearing black glasses?"

"Yes. He's the shortest of all your guests, but none are very tall."

"That is my cousin Nassar," Mayoubi said. He looked at Mrs. Saks and smiled. "It was bad when you thought he was a terrorist," he said. "But you are even worse now."

"I heard what I heard," she said, crossing her arms and glaring at him.

"You heard what you thought," Mayoubi said. "My cousin owns a business at home and is here looking for new outlets. My cousin Nassar sells carpeting for business. He is not selling drugs, He is selling *rugs*."

"How do we know you aren't lying?" she said, her voice quieter.

"You can come to my home and look at my floors. They are covered with samples." He took out his wallet and pulled out a business card, "Here is his name. And right here, the card says 'Carpets and Rugs.'"

"The words do sound alike," Nodding said. "Especially when you're in another car."

He watched as Mrs. Saks examined the card and saw her face lose its colour. "Now I feel simply horrible," she said. "I went and made matters so much worse."

"It is no cause for worry," Mayoubi said. "David had this meeting so we could come together and talk."

"But that's just part of it," she said. "When I thought he said drugs I went inside right away quick and called the police."

"What?" Mayoubi said. "And you said to them my relative was selling drugs?"

"I called the officer who was here for the truck accident," she said. "He wrote down the information and said he would get right on it." She looked at Mayoubi and shrugged. "I'll call him first thing in the morning and explain."

"By then we could all be shot," Mayoubi said. "I watch the news on television too. The RCMP will not ignore such a report from you."

He looked at Nodding. "I must hurry and tell my guests what this woman has done."

He started for the door, then stopped and looked at Mrs. Saks. "From now, leave me, my family, and my guests alone. You interfere too much."

He slammed the front door as he left.

11: Mysterious ways

"Would it help to call the RCMP now?" Nodding said. "Do you re-member the officer's name?"

"I have no intention of calling," she said. "I never called in the first place."

"Why did you say you did? Poor Wissam is terrified."

"I would be too, if I had a houseful of drugs." She looked at Nod-ding. ""You didn't fall for that cockamamie lie about rugs, did you?"

"He showed you his cousin's card."

"I bet they're Oriental rugs too," she said, putting her index fin-ger to her lips and biting it gently. "It all fits. They get hashish from Egypt and heroin from China and ship it all here rolled up in rugs and carpets."

"This makes no sense. If you really think they're drug smugglers, why didn't you call the police like you said?"

"Because Elliot is watching them. I lied a little bit there, too. He was parked outside this evening, watching everything they were up to. I know how these things work. He'll call in for support when he's ready."

"But you don't know for sure if he's local police or RCMP, if either," Nodding said. "I'm so confused I don't know what to be-lieve."

"Did you notice him with the cheese, David? He didn't touch the local blue or the cheddar. They were too Canadian for him. He went straight for that foreign brie, just as I thought he would. It's all fitting into place."

"Mrs Saks—"

"Leave it to me," she said, standing up. "Those monsters will be terrified tonight. I wouldn't be surprised if they tried to sneak their drugs out of the house before morning. But I'll be watching."

She patted Nodding on the shoulder and put on her coat. "Now, don't you worry, David. It's all under control. And thank you for the wine. I really ought to get a bottle to have on hand, in case anyone drops by."

She opened the door, peered out, and nodded. "The coast is clear. Goodnight, dear."

She closed the door softly behind her.

"She's crazy," Nodding told his living room. He pulled out his phone and tapped Wissam's number.

Mayoubi answered on the first ring. "Oh, David. I was expecting someone else."

"I'm so sorry, Wissam. I made it worse than it was before."

"The lady is a danger."

"She didn't call the police today," Nodding said. "She was lying about that part."

"Are you positive?" Mayoubi covered the telephone and said something, and then was back. "My guests think there will be a raid any minute."

"No raid is coming. I'll talk with her tomorrow, and I'll be sure to pass along anything you should know. But right now she hasn't done anything."

"Then we can all sleep tonight. Thank you, David. I do not blame you for this, you know. The woman is crazy."

Nodding hung up and put the dishes in his dishwasher. By morning he might have a full load. He shook his head and wondered if the water had something weird in it. Everyone was acting nuts. "And if they all think they're normal, what do they think of me?"

He looked at the dishwasher, as if expecting an answer. When none came, he felt a little relieved and went to bed.

Wednesday morning, Nodding woke up early and watched the news while he dressed. *There may be no wars going on*, he thought, *but people are still being killed all over the world*. He listened to a retired soldier and a professor from Halifax disagree about the wisdom of foreign involvement and thought about his own role as he sipped his coffee.

He didn't feel as bad about his shortcomings as a mediator and caught himself whistling as went down the steps to his car.

When he got to his office he checked his voicemail for messages, but there were none. It was still quiet in the cafeteria, so he typed up an angry email to the insurance adjuster and sent it off.

Then he walked up to the accounting office. There was no sign of Jenny.

"David!" Audrey Katz stood up at her desk and waved him over. "I just got in and buzzed your office, but you weren't there."

"Is Jenny here yet?"

"I knew it was early but I hoped maybe you'd be here. I just had your office extension and not your cell number."

She reached out and grabbed his wrist with her bony hand. "She's in hospital, David. He hit her too hard and broke a rib. There was some internal bleeding, so they're keeping her for a day, just in case."

"He broke a rib?" he said. "I almost came up to see her yesterday but I thought I should let things calm down."

"That's what I was trying to call you about. Jenny said not to come to the hospital. They haven't found Conrad yet, and she thinks he'll watch for you. She said to stay away and keep safe."

"This is ridiculous. He belongs in jail."

"I agree," Audrey said. "I'm going over to see her after work this afternoon."

She handed him a slip of paper. "Here's her number. But don't go over there, honey, for her sake. It'll just upset her more. I'll see her later and call you this evening, if you give me your number."

"You're right," he said. He took out his wallet and handed her a business card with his number. "I'll be home all evening."

"At least she told the police this time," Audrey said, putting the card in her purse. She opened a desk drawer and stuffed the purse inside. "She's safe now. Once they catch Conrad, anyway."

"Tell her I want to come see her," Nodding said.

He tucked the slip of paper with Jenny's number into his shirt pocket and went back to the cafeteria. Kwasi was checking the suggestion box by the door.

"Copy room sent down a fax for you," he said. "It oughta make your day."

Nodding went to his office and found the paper on his desk:

> *Called the office yesterday.*
> *Said your check is on its way.*
> *Hope this leaves you feeling fine.*
> *Poetically yours, Rich Valentine.*

"Now he must be a piece of work," Kwasi said, leaning in the door. "But at least your check isn't sitting on someone's desk."

"You don't appreciate accident report poetry?" Nodding said. "It's a very specialized field"

"Yeah. Hey, how'd your meeting go last night?"

"I shouldn't have gotten involved. Talk about traps."

"You're doing something," Kwasi said. "Long as you recognize it's a trap, it can't bite you."

"Sure isn't working like I planned."

"No guarantees," Kwasi said, shrugging.

"Hey, can I ask you a favour?"

"Shoot."

"Can I borrow your car until noon? I don't want anyone to see mine coming."

"Old lady Katz told me," Kwasi said. "This is the trap that's gonna get you nailed, Nodding."

He reached into his pocket and tossed his car key to Nodding. "But wait a minute."

He ducked out of the doorway, then returned in a minute with a white server's jacket. "Wear this and park in the emergency lot."

He pulled an electric food thermometer out of his pocket and handed it to Nodding. "Stick this in your coat pocket. Just don't let any of the nurses look at you too carefully, man."

Kwasi's red BMW started smoothly, and Nodding was impressed with the quiet engine. He turned down the radio, but the engine noise was still minimal. His Forester would go anywhere, but the engine was audible.

There were no strange cars near the gate or on the drive to St. Martha's Hospital. He gunned the BMW past the visitor's parking lot, resisting the urge to look for Conrad. Besides, he realized suddenly, he'd never even seen Conrad.

Pulling up to the emergency entrance, he parked in a "Doctors Only" space and headed into the hospital. A nurse at the counter, talking with an elderly woman, glanced up as he walked by, then went back to her conversation.

He went on to the main information desk, typed in Jenny's name, and went up to her room on the third floor. He half expected to see a policeman at the door, but the hallway was empty.

The room door was open. Jenny was sitting up, but asleep.

"Hi," he said, but she didn't wake up.

He wanted to walk over to the bed and gently stroke her face, which looked so calm. There were no bruises on her face at all.

He stepped over to the bed and took her hand, gently squeezing it. It was warm and soft, and he remembered how cold it had been in the cafeteria only a few days ago.

"David," she said, opening her eyes and looking around quickly. "You shouldn't be here."

"Audrey tried to keep me away," he said. "How are you feeling?"

"They told me the bleeding has stopped," she said. She reached over for her water cup and took a sip. "But the doctor wants to keep me here until tomorrow."

"Where will you go?"

"Not back there. Audrey says I can stay with her for a while. I'll be okay."

"Can I get you anything?"

"Thanks for coming, even though you're crazy," she said, squeezing his hand. "You need to get back to work. I'm fine, really."

"Can I call you tonight?" He let go of her hand and she smiled.

"I'd like that. But you have to be careful. Conrad bought a gun somewhere, an ugly little pistol."

"I don't even know what he looks like."

"He doesn't know what you really look like, either. He wanted me to tell him last night, after he beat me up."

"Sounds like he's really looking for me."

"I lied to him," she said. "I told him you looked like a nerd and wore glasses." She smiled a little. "You don't look like a nerd. But watch out for him. He's skinny, real pale, and has brown hair hanging to his shoulders. He always wears black jeans and drives a dark blue Jetta."

"Whoa," Nodding said. "I think he knows where I live. My neighbour saw a blue car hanging around our parking area."

He looked at her reaction. "I shouldn't have told you that."

"Call the RCMP," she said. "Let them deal with him if you see him or his car."

He smiled and went to the door, seeing her fade back to sleep.

Nodding got to the cafeteria just before the lunch rush and tossed Kwasi's keys back to him with a wink. When the rush was over, he went back to his office to check for messages.

There was some confusion about the coffee order, so he called and straightened it out. He had just hung up when a cook leaned in and said a driver wanted to talk to the boss. Nodding said to send him in; complaints were part of the job.

When the driver arrived, he glanced over and saw the boots. White crosses on the toes.

"Toby!" Nodding stood and came around his desk to shake hands. "I was going to call you today. What are you doing up here?"

"Jesus loves you, son," Toby said, squeezing his hand. "But we gotta talk, Dave."

"I got a message about the check." Nodding waved Toby to a chair. "It's supposed to be on the way."

"I'm glad. I didn't even get the right name to call out west. Can we close this door?"

"Sure." Nodding gave the door a push, then sat in his own chair while Toby settled back in the chair for visitors.

"Let me ask you something," Toby said. "Where did you say your friend saw that truck? The one she thought said Milker."

"Right next door to my townhouse."

"I got to Hagan. He buried his mother Monday and was already gonna be on the road today, God bless him. Told me he just had to get on the road and find some good french fries, but I expect he felt the need to get busy."

He took off his baseball cap and rubbed the rim. "Dave, there isn't any such company as Milker, like I thought. Your neighbour saw a Melchior rig, and none of them were supposed to be north of the 102. Hagan checked and called me back. I could barely understand him because he was chewing a doughnut from Tim's while we talked."

"That would explain why the driver took off after hitting her car. He wasn't supposed to be here."

"It's worse than that, buddy." Toby said. "None of their drivers could fake a detour and get away with it. Those are bonded drivers, on account of what they carry. The one in your lot was the one Hagan told us about. Remember?"

He saw Nodding's blank expression. "That truck was loaded with explosives and hijacked near Wolfville two weeks ago. It could have blown your whole neighbourhood to smithereens."

"Then Mrs. Saks must be right," Nodding said. "Here I thought she was crazy."

"Listen," Toby said. "Hagan had a run to the Valley this morning. I gave him your address and number. He told me he'd call if he found out anything else. And he has clearance to swing up here after delivery to show your neighbour a Melchior trailer. If that's what she saw, we'll have to call in the Mounties, pronto."

"I'll call her. It's only five minutes from here. I want to get to her first. If she sees Hagan before we talk to her, she could do something dangerous."

"He does present a poor first impression," Toby said, standing up.

"Didn't you have to work today?" Nodding said. "Her line's busy."

"Our Lord works in mysterious ways. They fired me yesterday."

"What? That's horrible. Why?"

"Because of the wreck," he said. "But it set me free to come over here. I haven't had time to get upset about it yet."

"Can I help?" Nodding asked. "Who could I call?" Mrs. Saks's number was still busy.

"Any answer?"

"No. Let's go," Nodding said, hanging up his desk phone.

He waved at Kwasi as he led Toby out to the parking lot. He started toward his car, but Toby pointed at a red pickup truck parked in the fire zone.

They climbed in, their breath clouding the front windshield at once. Nodding reached to wipe his side with his hand.

"Wait," Toby said, reaching over and laying his hand on Nodding's shoulder. "Lord Jesus, we know you're busy, what with all the suffering in the world, but we ask for your protection and guidance today. Help us keep them explosives out of the hands of crazy people. Amen."

"Amen," said Nodding.

12: Big time action in Antigonish

"Fasten your seat belt," Toby said. "I forgot to pray for my driving."

The truck roared to life and Toby put it in gear. "This is left over from my wilder days. I peeled off the beer decals, but it still runs good"

He had a small plastic Jesus glued to the dashboard that swayed a bit and seemed to crouch a bit as Toby sped up. "There's a little crack in his legs," Toby said, glancing at the statue. He looked back at the street as Nodding directed him.

They turned into the townhouse development and sped to Nodding's street. Facing them and parked in front of Nodding's house was a white truck with an unmarked gray tractor.

"Is that Hagan?" Nodding asked.

"Jesus Lord," Toby said, slowing down. "That ain't a Melchior rig. You can always tell Hagan's tractor because he has a naked woman statue glued where I keep Jesus. Look at those fellas loading crates."

"Park anywhere and we can go to my place. I don't recognize these guys. We can call the police and hope nothing blows up before they get here."

Toby swung into a parking space several homes down from Nodding's. They climbed out and tried not to hurry as they walked.

Nodding noticed the white cars had shifted down to make room for the truck and that one of them was in his parking spot. He also saw the black car Mrs. Saks was using was in her usual parking space.

"Morning, fellas," Toby said, waving to two men carrying crates toward the truck. "Sure is a cold one."

The men smiled and nodded, but said nothing.

"Bless you now," said Toby as they reached the steps to Nodding's door.

"Calm down," he said quietly as Nodding fumbled to open his front door. "God's hand is with us, and He won't let us fail."

The door opened and Nodding's phone started ringing. He answered it while Toby shut the door,

"David, it worked," Mrs. Saks said. "They're loading their drugs."

"Stay inside," Nodding said. "I'll talk to you later." He hung up and tapped 911.

"Listen." Toby pulled the curtains back and looked out. The truck had started and was revving its engine. "Guy don't know how to drive."

"Send a car," Nodding said. "We need help." He put down the phone, knowing the police computer would know his address.

"They're fixing to leave," Toby said, letting go of the curtain. "Guide me into the lion's den, sweet Jesus," He pulled down his baseball cap and jerked open the door.

"Wait," Nodding said, following him outside.

"In the name of the Lord God, you men stop." Toby raised both hands above his head and looked down at the truck.

A man closing the trailer doors stopped and looked up. Another man standing next to the cab turned to stare. Wissam Mayoubi came around the front of the truck and shook his head.

"David, you should not have come out," he said. He stood at the foot of the steps to Nodding's door.

"You can't get away with this, Wissam. The police are coming."

"That is why everyone is leaving," Mayoubi said. "We would have shipped these boxes later, but I saw the man in the blue car watching. We had to move faster."

"You said he was a rug dealer," Nodding said, listening for sirens.

"But he is," Wissam said. "They took the wrong truck. It made all these problems for us. You cannot sell explosives like you can sell rugs. So we had to sell to these men."

He shook his head and looked over as his cousin and guests came out of the townhouse carrying suitcases. He waved at them to hurry. "This mess has made me into a criminal so I must run and hide. But at least I will have enough money."

"The police will catch you," Toby said. "Put down your guns and give up."

"We have no guns," Wissan said. "I sell computer parts. My relatives steal rugs. We need no guns."

He saw Toby look at Nodding. "But the men in the truck have guns. Be safe, David. Just stay back until we are gone."

He waved at his cousin, who ran over and handed him a briefcase. "Tell them to get going," Wissam said. "The truck is blocking our cars."

Nassar turned and waved at the truck, which lurched forward.

"Jesus, are you watching?" Toby said. "I fear no evil."

"Tell Mrs. Saks it was a pleasure," Wissam said, turning and stepping into the street. "I left her a rug in my living room."

"Any time, sweet Lord," Toby said. "We're ready." There were still no sirens. "We can stop, them, Dave. The guys with guns are leaving."

"Wissam. Wissam." Nassar had stopped by a white car and was pointing down the street. A Melchior truck had swung around the corner and stopped, blocking the exit. The white truck came to a halt.

"Hagan," Nodding said.

"Thank you, Jesus," Toby said, lifting his arms in the air. "Right on the button."

"This is not fair!" Wissam said. He threw his briefcase onto the seat of the car in Nodding's spot and climbed in, fumbling with his keys.

Down the street there was a loud boom. Nodding saw Hagan standing beside his truck, holding a shotgun. He was aiming it at the other truck and yelling.

"Wissam, Wissam!" Nassar had climbed out of his car and was waving his keys at his cousin. "Wrong cars. I need your keys." He reached over the roof of the white car between them, waving his car keys with one hand and pushing up his glasses with the other.

Nodding realized the man wasn't wearing a coat.

"Don't you try to run from me, shithead!" Everyone turned to see a wiry young man spring from behind a blue Jetta across the street. He was waving a pistol at Nassar, who saw him and dove to the pavement. The first shot exploded the white rental's rear window.

"Time to pray," Toby said, pulling Nodding down. "Sweet Jesus."

Wissam had opened his car door and was stepping out when Conrad's shot hit the car beside him. He saw Conrad swing the gun in his direction and ducked down.

"The key," he yelled under the car.

Nassar stared at him wildly, then lurched up and began to crawl toward the front of the car.

"I knew you'd run, you chickenshit," Conrad said, stepping over to see between the cars. He fired another shot as Nassar dove to the front of the rental. The gun made little popping sounds as it fired. "Jenny Sue belongs to me, you hear?"

His third shot hit the car's trunk with a thud, sending Wissam crawling forward to huddle with his cousin in front of the car.

Conrad moved forward and stared, and they all heard the sirens. "No damned cops can keep me from my woman."

"Young man?"

Conrad turned, pointing the gun at Mrs. Saks. He was standing beside her black rental, and she had rolled down the driver's side window.

"Behave now," she said.

Conrad looked at her blankly, then fired three shots at the pavement under Nassar's rental. Wissam and Nassar floundered away from the car as bullets hit, crawling quickly down the sidewalk toward Wissam's townhouse.

Conrad raised his gun and pulled the trigger, but the pistol was empty. He quickly reached into his pocket and pulled out a handful of bullets, as Nassar and Wissam stood up and began to run down the sidewalk toward the trucks and sirens.

"Drop it or you're history, Elliot," Mrs. Saks said.

Conrad looked to see her hand reaching out of her car window, only ten feet away. The Luger was aiming at his belly. She lowered the gun slightly.

"You think you scare me, old lady?" he said, fumbling with his pistol.

"I should hope so," she said, raising the pistol.

He looked at it closely, then dropped his gun and the bullets and ran, ducking around the side of her townhouse and not looking back.

"Sweet Jesus, Hallelujah!" Toby yelled. "We have been delivered." He grabbed Nodding and hugged him, pulling him to his feet.

Mrs. Saks left her gun in the car and was heading across the street toward them. Toby hurried over and gave her a hug. "The Lord has sent us an angel," he said, then turned to watch the arriving police cars.

Mrs. Saks shook her head at him and shrugged. "David, who was that man I thought was Elliot? If I had known he wasn't a policeman I would never have hidden. I might have been hurt."

"Are you okay, Mrs. Saks?" Nodding tried to stop her, but she stalked towards the damaged car.

"Just look at this mess," she said, peering at the hole in the trunk. "Thank goodness it's only a rental."

She turned to Nodding. "This isn't yours, is it?".

"No, mine's at work."

"And who is this man who keeps screaming?" she said, pointing at Toby.

Nodding realized Toby had started down toward the trucks, where policemen were fanning out behind the townhouses, and Hagan was moving to meet him.

"That's Toby," he said. "If you're okay, I'll head down there."

"I love excitement," she said. "I just wish I had some bullets." She turned to peer at the car's broken rear window.

"Hey, Nodding." Hagan was walking with Toby back towards him. He had turned over his shotgun to the police, but was wearing a white cowboy hat. "You boys throw one helluva a welcome party, let me tell you."

He spat, then shook Nodding's hand. "Damnation, I near to shit when I saw that rig coming toward me. Didn't know what to do when that goon jumped out with a pistol, so I grabbed old Lucy and fired a round out my window. Damn sucker wet his pants and throwed up his hands right then. All I could think of was a bullet sparking in that trailer and we'd all be on our way to the clouds."

"The Lord answered our prayers when you showed up," Toby said. "Even I was a bit worried about his timing, "

"Lord had nothin' to do with it," Hagan said. "You called me and I said I was coming. I even wore my old man's Gunsmoke hat. I figured it oughta see some excitement, but I had no idea we'd have High Noon right here in Antigonish. If I'd had any notion I would have driven a tank down the street."

"I guess the RCMP will have some questions for us," Toby said, watching the truck driver being led away in handcuffs.

"I'll get Mrs. Saks," Nodding said. He hurried back across the street through the gathering neighbours who had begun to emerge and found Mrs. Saks wiping off her pistol with a rag from the trunk of her rental car.

"I want it to look good," she said. "I know the police will take it away from me since it isn't registered. But I want them to see it was taken care of."

"Let's leave it here with the car and walk up the street," Nodding said. "We don't want the police to think you're about to shoot any-one."

"Heavens, I never thought of that," she said, putting down the gun at once. "Did they capture all of the smugglers?"

"They have the guys from the truck and some of Wissam's friends. They're still looking for the man you scared away."

Toby was waiting with a detective when they got near the trucks. "They're getting a statement from Hagan up by his tractor," he said. "Guess this is all a mite complicated. They picked up that little guy with the glasses running down the middle of the street. They're still looking for the guy with the name Whizzam? They think he might have doubled back behind the houses, so they're looking hard back there."

"You'd think the guy would want to get as far from here as pos-sible," the detective said, checking his cell phone. "He has to know we'll be searching every inch of his house."

"It's the money," Mrs. Saks said. "That's what he's after."

"Oh my God," Nodding said. "I didn't even think about it. But you're right. He threw that briefcase into the car and he didn't have it when he took off."

"Which car?" the detective asked. "Larry!"

A uniformed policeman came over and Nodding pointed out the car. The officer moved toward it.

"Perhaps I can take your statement now, before something else happens," the detective said. He led Nodding to a police car. Two other detectives came up to attend to Mrs. Saks and Toby.

It took Nodding almost an hour to explain everything he knew about the situation to the detective, whose name was Martin. "The trucker with the hat kept asking me if I was a cowboy," Martin said. "I told him one cowboy was enough in this neighbourhood. But I got to admit he stopped those bad boys dead in the road until we got here."

Nodding sat in the car while Martin compared notes with the other detectives. Finally they separated, and Martin came back to the car.

"Mr. Nodding, here's how it looks to us," he said. "Correct me if I miss something. Mayoubi and his buddies thought they were stealing rugs. A bedroom in that townhouse has a whole stack of rugs, so that much makes sense. Have you been in there?"

"No," Nodding said. "And he's only been in my place once. We barely know each other."

"Good computer setup. He's hooked into some trucker networks so he could know what's going on."

"They could track rug shipments."

"But they screwed up and got some explosives," Martin said. "One of the guys, calls himself Nassar, said the plan was to ship them down to the States. But security is tight these days, so they dumped that plan. Then they hooked up with these guys who normally fence electronic goods. Strictly a half-ass operation, but they almost got away with it, except for that old lady. She's a piece of work. She keeps asking if we found the drugs, even after we explained it all to her. And who is this guy Elliot?"

"He's the guy who shot at the car," Nodding said.

"Real name Conrad."

"Right. She thought he was an undercover officer and called him Elliot."

"Well, she misunderstood the whole thing, but her instincts were right," Martin said. "She scared Conrad off before anyone got hurt. And that was good, since he was shooting at the wrong guy anyway."

He shook his head. "This is such a messed up kerfuffle. It's a miracle no one was killed."

"Did you catch Conrad?" Nodding asked.

"Not yet. But he's out there on foot somewhere, and we're looking. We missed Mayoubi too. He must have circled around and gone back to his car while everyone was running down here, and grabbed his money. The car door was open, and the briefcase was empty. But he's on foot, too. We'll find him."

"Is Mrs. Saks okay?"

"We convinced her to spend the night with a friend," Martin. said. "You going to be okay here?"

"I'm fine," Nodding said. "But I'll rest easier when I hear you have Conrad under arrest. So far he doesn't know what I look like. What's his last name, anyway?"

"That's it, according to his arrest record. He just goes by Conrad. With a first name like Mabou, I might, too. But we'll get him soon."

When Nodding finally climbed out of the car, it was beginning to get dark. Toby and Hagan were sitting on his steps, waiting, watching the policemen measure the parking lot and take photos of the rental cars.

"These guys are cranked up," Hagan said, standing and scratching his belly. "Big time action in Antigonish."

"Not much happens in this neighbourhood," Nodding said.

"Hell," Hagan said. "This is where it's at. Nothing like this happens anywhere in Nova Scotia."

"How about I order some pizza?" Nodding said. "I can make some coffee and I have beer, wine, and soda."

"Coffee sounds mighty good, Dave," Toby said. "It's getting cold out here."

"You got two hungry drivers to feed," Hagan said. "Let's order some fries with them pizzas. But no anchovies on the pizza. If I want seafood, I'll find me some fresh haddock or scallops."

13: Is this a test?

Nodding called in the order and put on the coffee while Toby and Hagan took off their coats and sat down. When the first few cups were brewed, Nodding carried them into the living room.

"Good and strong," Toby said. "Just what the body needs on a night like this."

"So, I never asked, Preacher," Hagan said, "but what the hell are you doing over this way?" He poured some coffee into his saucer and blew on it, then sipped from the saucer. "Don't tell me your wife lets you get out for some excitement now and then."

"I wasn't too far away," Toby said. "Dave needed some help."

"Wait a minute," Nodding said. He put down his coffee. "Back at the cafeteria you said you'd been fired. I forgot all about it."

"They said one crash was too many. God's will."

"Those shitheads," Hagan said, coffee dripping from his beard. "Too cheap to pay the higher insurance, so they ruin a man's life."

He wiped his chin on his flannel sleeve. "Well, Melchior needs a driver, but if this stuff today gets to you, I wouldn't take it. There's a reason I ride with my shotgun up front with me. When you haul dynamite all kinds of nut jobs get interested."

"I'm not sure what I'll do just yet," Toby said, draining his cup. "The union says they'll protest, but I gotta pay my bills in the meantime. Thought I'd check out moving companies. They'll be hiring once spring comes."

"Our food distributor lost a couple of drivers over the holidays,"

Nodding said. "I could ask when I call in an order."

"You see?" Toby smiled. "God will provide through friends like you guys. I'm hoping something will come up close to home. But if nothing does, you may hear from me. Car door outside. Hope it's the pizza, 'cause I best be heading home."

"Me too," Hagan said. The doorbell rang, and Nodding hurried to answer. He paid for the pizza, put it on the coffee table, then got plates and napkins from the kitchen.

"Some good," Hagan said, wiping a dribble of sauce from his chin. "Before we finish up, I want to tell you boys something. For once, I think I need to ask for some help, and I don't know who else to talk to."

"What's on your mind?" Toby said, putting down his pizza and leaning forward.

"First off, I appreciate your prayers for my ma, preacher. She was damn near as religious as you."

"I was sorry to hear about her passing," Nodding said. "Toby told me about it on the phone."

"We wasn't close," Hagan said, pushing a piece of pizza crust around his plate. "Hadn't seen her since my dad's funeral, almost nine years ago. Didn't approve of me, didn't like me driving truck, none of it. She owned this big old religious revival hotel on the ocean down in Port Medway. You would love it, Preacher."

"Was she ill, God rest her soul?" Toby said.

"Nope, healthy as a horse. She didn't drink or smoke, barely even drank coffee. But she did have one vice, and damned if it didn't do her in." He saw their looks. "Ma gambled. She bought three lottery tickets for every drawing. 'For Father, Son, and Holy Spirit,' she'd say."

"Amen," Toby said, folding his hands.

"This went on for years, like I say, because I haven't seen her."

"Did she lose everything?" Nodding asked.

"She won," Hagan said. "Hit that big lottery for eighty-three million, and damned if she wasn't the only winner. Got so worked up that she dropped dead right in the lottery office with the first check in her hand."

"Oh Lord," Toby said.

"Eighty-three million?" Nodding said.

"Bingo," Hagan said, smiling, "I'm her only kid, and she left everything to me. But, shit, there's a catch to this whole deal, and that's where I need some advice."

"You need a lawyer," Toby said. "I can't even imagine that much money, let alone trying to give advice about it. Jesus led a simple life, and I've been happy doing the same."

"Got a lawyer," Hagan said, running his fingers through his hair. He glanced at his fingers to see what might have brushed out. "Like I said, my mother didn't think much of me and what I've been doing. So she came up with this plan to convert me. I inherit all her property and money, but there's a catch. I have to keep her Bible resort running, or it and her money go to charity."

"Did she make up the will before the lottery?" Nodding said.

"Oh yeah," Hagan said."See, she figured I'd have to give up driving and move down there to run the centre, since it barely broke even. Only way I'd be able to get anything would be to hang out with the Jesus freaks for two years. No offence, Preacher."

"No finer people," Toby said. "But I understand."

"After two years I could sell the place. Hell, it'd go for at least a million, so it would be worth my time running it. But now, shit, I can hire people to run it for me and have it done right."

"Sounds like you've got it made," Nodding said.

"I don't know," Hagan said. "I already got a call from the old biddy who worked with ma. She wouldn't speak to me at the funeral. Said she wasn't working for any devil-loving truck driver and would see to it her friends quit, too. Hell, I gotta have the place ready to open in May, boys, and I don't know shit about it."

"It's never too late to learn," Toby said. "God can be your guide."

"You don't get it, Preacher," Hagan said. "Ma knew I'd screw up and lose everything. I ain't cut out for running any hotel or food trough, much less a religious one. Ma wanted me to mess it up, and I would have, if I had to go down there and do it myself."

"Maybe she just wanted you to see the Light," Toby said. "I saw it in a parking lot in the middle of a storm."

"Just find some good people to run it for you," Nodding said. "Get a good manager and things will work out just fine."

"It hit me when we were waiting for the pizza," Hagan said. "You two could do it for me, and I could trust both of you."

"I'm a driver," Toby said. "I serve the Lord on the highway, but I wouldn't know squat about running a Bible Centre."

"You'd be fine, Toby," Nodding said. "I can help Hagan find a good manager to take care of the rooms and meals. But you've worked with your church. You can organize prayer meetings and services. Just get vacationing ministers to run the services and preach in exchange for a week's vacation. I bet you could attract some good ministers from other provinces."

"How'd you think of that?" Hagan said. "See, I knew you guys could help."

"When I was a kid our minister used to take a vacation and run services on PEI," Nodding said. "They do it all the time. Or you could get a retired minister from Ontario to come out here for a couple of weeks."

"I do organize our Bible Outreach," Toby said. "I'm pretty good at working with folks, but it's pretty informal. I just don't know."

"I'd pay you a good salary," Hagan said.

"I have a family," Toby said. "And a house and such. I'd dearly love to give it a try, but I've gotta be realistic."

"Shit on realistic," Hagan said. "Listen to me, Preacher. Realistic went in the hopper once Ma won that lottery. Nothin's real no more. This is Dreamland we're talking about, and chances like this don't come along twice. I can't let it pass. And I sure as hell can't do it alone."

"Look," Toby said, looking pained. "I'm interested, but I keep coming back to the Lord's prayer, where it says 'Lead us not into temptation,' and it scares me. You're talking about two summers of work. I can't uproot my family for that."

"If we can make it work, I won't sell it in two years," Hagan said. "I'll put that in writing. We can even expand it to a full year operation, if we think it will work. We could bring in church groups on weekends or give Boy Scouts or Girl Guides a place to go when it's too cold to go camping. I've been thinking about this. Them holy roller groups are always looking for a place to let loose, and we can give it to them." He ran a hand through his beard. "I get all worked up just thinking about it. Shit."

There was a pause while all three ran ideas through their minds and searched for traps. Then Hagan said, "Preacher, there's a house my Ma lived in right there on the property. You can live there rent-free, so you don't have to give up your present house. Hell, I can even throw in money so you can take winter courses in Bible studies if you want."

"Is this a test of my faith?" Toby said. "It looks too good to be real."

"I need you, Preacher," Hagan said. "Can you imagine me with a hotel full of Girl Guides? That's what temptation is all about, and I know I'd mess up. I'm asking you to do the job right, and I trust you. I won't be there to get in your way."

There was one piece of pizza left, and Hagan picked it up and stuffed half of it into his mouth. Some sauce dripped onto his hand, and he wiped it on his jeans.

"What do you plan to do yourself?" Nodding said.

"I'll keep my license, just in case. But I have some thinking to do. The wife is already planning a fancy house and pool, but I ain't cut out for no golf course life, that much I do know."

"Can I pray on this tonight?" Toby said. "I want to talk with my family, too."

"Of course," Hagan said. "I may head down there this weekend to check things out. Gotta meet with the solicitor, too, so there ain't that big a rush." He looked at Nodding. "I meant what I said, Dave. I don't know you too good, but if you're good enough for the university, I'll make it worth your while to move."

"I don't think so," Nodding said. "But thanks. I've just too much happening here right now. But I'll get you in touch with a few people who could do the job."

"I don't want people, I want you," Hagan said. "You know what I'm like, and we can talk okay eyeball to eyeball. That's what I need."

He stood up and offered his hand. "Once I figure things out a little more, I'm gonna call you and try to change your mind."

He shook hands with Toby, then reached for his jacket. "I'm blocking half the street out there, so I'd best get moving. Thinking about cruising over to Mother Webb's for a steak before I get on the road. Don't get this close very often."

"Check it out carefully," Nodding said. "Do it everywhere you eat, so you know what to tell your manager you want."

"Damn." Hagan said. "Guess I gotta start thinking different."

"Next time you're in Truro, stop in at the Paradise Lodge," Nodding said. "Rooms are nice, and the food is simple, tasty, and not expensive. Good menu choices."

"Can't," Hagan said. "I've seen that place before, but coming through there yesterday it was closed up. Shut down."

"I just stayed there last week," Nodding said, remembering the girl.

"They had special drivers' rates," Toby said. "But it's too close to home for me to stop."

"I heard them chatting about it on the radio," Hagan said. "Said Paradise was sealed tight. Couldn't get in."

"Any mention of an angel with a sword?" Toby said. "Maybe out in the garden?"

"You have too much coffee, Preacher?" Hagan said. "Didn't hear no such thing. One guy said the parking lot was chained off, but he didn't mention no guards or garden."

"Oh well," Toby said.

"I gotta go," Hagan said. "I'll watch for good places to eat."

"I don't know how to thank you," Nodding said. "You showed up at the nick of time."

"Amen, brother," Toby said, pulling on his coat. "I'll call you tomorrow, Hagan."

He grabbed Nodding's shoulder and squeezed.

"Thanks. Toby."

"Need a lift back to your car?" Toby said. "We came over here in a bit of a hurry."

"Don't worry. I'll get someone to pick me up in the morning," Nodding said.

Hagan opened the door left. Toby and Nodding followed him, only to find Mrs. Saks climbing the steps.

"I was hoping you were home, David, after this climb." She stepped to the side to let Hagan and Toby pass her on the steps. "You fellows did a fine job today," she said. She patted Hagan on the shoulder as he passed. "Nice shooting."

"Just popped one off at the sky," he said. "Heard you handled that pistol with style."

He waved at Nodding and went down the street toward his truck, while Toby stopped by Mrs. Saks.

"Will you be all right here, dear?" he asked. "We heard you were staying with a friend."

"Her idea of excitement is a warm pierogi," Mrs, Saks said. "I'm nobody's dear and I wouldn't be anywhere else tonight."

"Jesus loves you," Toby said, heading down the steps. "I'll call you, Dave."

14: The best thing for you

"He the one who hit your car?" Mrs. Saks said. "Or is it that man with food all over his coat?"

"It was me," Toby said, opening the door to his truck. "Guess I won't ever forget that night. Not now." He climbed in and started the engine.

"They both seem nicer than that idiot who hit my Buick," Mrs. Saks said. "Is all the wine from last night gone, David?"

"There's still some left. These guys both had to drive, so they drank coffee. Come on in. I have to make a phone call quickly, but I'll get you a glass first."

He ushered Mrs. Saks into the living room, grabbed the plates and pizza box, and took them to the kitchen. He brought back a glass of wine while she took off her coat.

"No one touched the blue cheese last night," he said. "Would you like some?"

"It looked a bit spicy to me," she said. "I'm full from dinner any-way. Dolores made a chicken pot pie and I had seconds. This non-sense today left me starving."

"I'll be right back," Nodding said. He ducked into his bedroom, found the number on his phone, and called the hospital. The oper-ator connected him, and Audrey Katz picked up the telephone.

"Jenny's asleep," she said. "You snuck out here already, David."

"Just for a few minutes," he said. "How is she?"

"A police officer was here. She told Jenny about Conrad shooting at you, and she's worried sick to death."

"He wasn't shooting at me. Tell her the phony description worked. When will she get out?"

"They think tomorrow," Audrey said. "I'm taking her to my place for a few days to fatten her up, poor darling. She needs some casseroles to put a little meat on those ribs."

"We'll have to find her a place to stay," Nodding said. "You can't put her up forever."

"I'd better hang up. You be careful, David. The police are keeping an eye on the hospital, so Jenny's safe and sound."

"Tell her I called," Nodding said. He hung up and hurried back to the living room.

"Someone sick?" Mrs. Saks asked. She had moved from the couch to the easy chair to be closer to the bedroom door. Nodding noticed her wine glass was empty, brought the bottle from the kitchen and poured the remains into her glass.

"The guy you called Elliot was looking for me," he said. "He thinks I'm trying to steal his girlfriend and he's nuts. He beat her up last night, and she's in the hospital."

"Oh dear," Mrs. Saks said. "This is worse than I thought."

"I think things will work out. At least she's away from him."

"Well, you bring that poor dear over to meet me when she's better, David. If I had any inkling Elliot was a woman beater I'd have blown him to kingdom come."

"Then you'd be in trouble, Mrs. Saks," he said. "I'm glad you didn't have bullets."

"This bought us some time, David, but those terrorists are tough cookies. They aren't out of the picture yet, you mark my words."

"Maybe not, but now the police can handle everything. We've done all we can."

"Well, let's wait and see about that," she said. "You don't know these people, David. I saw a special on the cable. Mr. Mayoubi will be like a terrier with a rat."

She drained her glass and stood up. "He'll be back, and I'll be ready this time."

"What does that mean?" Nodding said, helping her on with her coat.

"Loose lips sink ships," she said. "Thank you, David. I really will hurry up and buy some of that wine for myself."

Nodding escorted her down the steps and across the street. The night was clear and cold and the fresh air felt good. When he got back to his living room he thought about watching the news to see if they mentioned the afternoon excitement but he was tired. Instead, he glanced at his mail and found a cheque from the trucking company for his car.

He stuck the wine glass in the dishwasher with the pizza plates and coffee cups, checked the chain on his front door, and went to bed.

The next morning Nodding called the university, and a security guard drove over and gave him a ride to the cafeteria. Before he went into his office and had to tell his story, he got into the white rental car and drove it over to Tip-Top.

"Mr. Nodding," Stan said. "Was there any damage to this car in all your excitement?"

"No. How'd you hear about it?"

"You made the news. And then the media sites are full of talk and pictures. The police towed our cars to their lot to process them for evidence, and I saw one of the white Hyundais had some damage."

"Everything's fine with mine," Nodding said. "It's a nice little car."

"Can you believe it?" Stan said. "Mr. Mayoubi called this morning and told me to pick up the cars. He didn't want his credit card charged for any more days."

"Did you call the police?"

"They're already watching the building. They think he might stop in. This is like television."

"Well, one experience like that is enough for me," Nodding said. He signed the papers Stan offered and handed over his key.

"Funny thing is, it's been good for business," Stan said. "I got three calls already this morning for rentals. Can you believe it? I had to call to the airport for more cars."

"Well, good luck," Nodding said. "Thanks again."

In the hallway he noticed a man with a mop who waved a hand radio at him and nodded. Nodding was happy to get out to the street and enjoyed the brief walk to Auto Body Shop.

"Hey David, you're famous now," Nick said, getting up from his desk. Nodding looked over at the bathroom, which had an "Out of Order" sign on the door.

"I hope not for long," he said. "Your cheque finally came."

"I washed your Forester first thing today." Vincent said he saw the story on the news. Those guys are still on the loose, eh?"

"A couple of them."

"That you, David?"

Nodding turned at the voice and saw the new speaker and camera mounted above the bathroom door.

"Hi, Vincent. You out in the truck?"

"It's great," Vincent said. "I'd invite you out, but it's still pretty messy. Once I get some tires on and wheel it out front, I can put in a couch for guests. I'll give you a call then and you can come visit."

"I can't wait to see it when it's finished," Nodding said. He handed the cheque to Nick.

"We gotta move the speaker to a better place," Nick said. "Yesterday Vincent heard it every time someone had to go, you know? Once it even happened during his lunch, and that kind of thing can ruin your appetite."

"I asked Nick, 'Put up a sign,' but he forgot yesterday. I called out to him just as one old man was using the toilet. I scared him pretty bad, I guess. He thought the light fixture was talking to him. Boy, what a mess."

"Maybe you could play some music in there, to cover the noise," Nodding said.

"It's all set," Nick said, handing him the keys. "I'll open the shop doors for you. I parked it inside to keep it nice and warm." He glanced at the bathroom. "I'm going into the shop now Vincent. David is getting his Forester."

"I'll see you soon, David. Anything wrong, you bring it back to us."

"I will," he said. "Thanks, Vincent."

"And come visit. I got an espresso maker in here all ready to be set up. I'll give you a call, you come celebrate my new office."

The Forester smelled like cigar smoke but it looked like new. Nodding backed out carefully, then put down the windows as he returned to work. By the time he got to the university, he had rolled the windows back up.

"The office called," Kwasi said as Nodding came in. "Said to tell you the administration appreciates the fact you didn't mention the university in any interviews."

"I never even thought about it," Nodding said, hanging up his coat.

"You got everyone talking. Old Austi came in a half hour early today. She nearly died when you weren't here and there was nothing to do but start working."

"Any word from Audrey?" Nodding glanced at his desk phone, but the message light wasn't lit.

"Oh yeah," Kwasi said. "She dropped off a recipe for onion soup and said Conrad was still on the loose. Said she'd be back at lunch."

"That it?"

"Nothing about our Ms. Porter. Hey, I'm glad you're okay, Nodding. No one else around here puts up with my talks on philosophy."

"No one else falls into the traps, either," Nodding said.

They spent the rest of the morning discussing food delivery schedules and whether or not to expand the vending machine offerings. When Kwasi got up to help with the lunch line, Nodding noticed Audrey Katz eating a salad at a window table.

"I'm glad I remembered," she said when he came out. "Don't even try that onion soup recipe. Throw it away."

"Why?" he said, trying to remember where he put it.

"I realized I wrote it down all wrong. I looked at my copy when I went back to my desk, and it says to add one tablespoon of salt. I'm sure I wrote down one cup. I'll make you a new copy."

"I probably would have caught it. How's Jenny?"

"I was worried sick you'd already be trying it," she said. "People would see my name on the recipe bulletin board and they'd never trust me again."

"Don't worry," he said, "We're not that fast. We'll try it in a couple of weeks, and we'll get the salt right."

"I was just nervous, that's all. I didn't sleep too well, what with Jenny in the hospital and seeing you on the news."

"Is she getting out today?"

"She already is," Audrey said. "She called. The police said they'd drive her to my place and make sure she got settled safely. She said she'd call later."

She pushed some salad around her plate. "This fat-free ranch dressing just doesn't taste good. I miss that mayonnaise touch."

"We have regular dressing, too. When you take out the fat, you lose the good flavour."

"Have you tried that fat-free margarine?" she said. "I keep thinking, what's the point? If you don't want fat, don't eat margarine.

But I don't mind the reduced-fat spread. It tastes just like butter on baked potatoes. You don't even need sour cream, which is good. Low fat sour cream reminds me of white gelatin."

She put down her fork and looked fixedly at him. "David, the best thing for you would be to marry Jenny and take good care of her."

"I haven't even gone out with her. I've only eaten lunch with her twice, and that was here."

"Get a move on, then. She needs someone to take care of her, poor dear, and not an old lady like me. We'll drive each other crazy in that mobile home before long."

"I'll call her tonight," he said.

"You could stop by. I'll make some dip and you two can talk. I'll even go out to the movies."

"No. She just got out of the hospital. Let her take it easy tonight. We'll see how she feels tomorrow."

"Oh, you're right," she said. "Anyway, I better get back to my desk. But before I leave I'm going to buy a candy bar. This low-fat nonsense takes all the fun out of eating. Tomorrow I'm going to eat a sandwich and enjoy every mouthful."

Nodding took her tray to the dishroom while Audrey stopped by the vending machines.

15: Heavy laden

"I gotta ask," Kwasi said, coming up to Nodding near his office. "Who was the dude yesterday with white crosses on his boots? I saw him on the news talking to some cops."

"Toby?" Nodding smiled. "He's the trucker who hit my car."

"Sometime you have to tell me the whole story. I can't even begin to guess how your wreck ties in with a truckload of explosives."

"It gets weirder. What if I told you it leads to a job opening as manager of a conference centre with a salary better than working here?"

"You looking?"

"I was thinking of you," Nodding said. "Full responsibility for the hotel and food operation."

"There's gotta be a catch," Kwasi said. "Otherwise, you'd go for it yourself."

"It's a religious conference centre over on the South Shore. Toby, the guy with crosses on his boots, may run the religious meetings and oversee the services."

"A truck driver? Who the hell would hire him for that job?"

"Well, it's owned by another driver who just inherited it from his mother. He needs some help with the place."

"It's a career trap, if not suicide," Kwasi said. "No thanks, man. I want out of the kitchen and into an office for my next job. My next boss will ask me to play golf in the afternoon, not help him lube up his eighteen wheeler for fun."

"I didn't think you'd be interested, but I thought I'd mention it."

"I appreciate it. But don't you start thinking about it, either. That's a trap you won't get out of in one piece. Anywhere in that area except one of the tourist resorts is a step down, and you know it."

"Yeah," Nodding said. "But if it worked out it could help with a job at one of the resorts."

"Dreaming," Kwasi said, heading back to the kitchen. "You're spending too much time with truckers. You're better off with Jenny Porter."

Nodding went into his office, where he managed to work quietly for the rest of the day. When he left for home it was already dark.

He drove over to the grocery store, noting that the cigar smell had already faded in his car. At the market, he picked up enough to get through the weekend, then strolled over to the mall, where he turned off his cell phone and wandered for awhile, glancing at people who didn't recognize him.

Then he went out and walked over to a favourite restaurant, where he ordered a steak. He had a beer, ate a small Caesar salad, and enjoyed a baked potato with sour cream. By the time he finished his steak, he felt fine and left for home.

The parking lot was quiet. Wissam's house was dark, and a police tape still fluttered across the door. Mrs. Saks was home, but her curtains were drawn.

Nodding went inside, turned on some lights, and switched on his cell phone.

"Hi, David, this is Jenny. I'm at Audrey's place and everything is fine. I told Audrey I was going to work tomorrow. I have the whole weekend to rest up afterwards, and I'm tired of sitting around. Anyway, I wondered if we could eat lunch together. I'll see you tomorrow. Bye."

Nodding thought about calling right away but decided to wait.

There was another message anyway.

"Jesus works His blessings for us all," Toby's voice said. "I was reading the Good Book late last night, and I came on this here line in Matthew: 'For I was hungry, and ye gave me meat, I was thirsty and ye gave me drink, I was a stranger and ye took me in.' and it got me to thinking. So I kept going and it says: 'Inasmuch as ye have done it unto one of the least of these my brethren, ye have done it unto me.' Don't that send chills right up your spine? It's like Matthew was talking about the hotel business, just to me. But I want to talk with you one more time before I call Hagan, if you don't mind. So feel free to call me at home or I'll try you again later. I don't think I can sleep tonight, I'm so worked up. I keep thinking of a big old hotel with a blue neon cross way up over it, you know, with 'JESUS SAVES' blinking out at the ocean. I'll talk with you soon, Dave. God loves you, buddy."

Nodding stared at his phone. For some reason he caught himself thinking back to his night at the Paradise Lodge. It had been so re-cent, yet it seemed so long ago. And now it was closed up. *How could it have changed so quickly?* But his life had changed just as quickly, he guessed.

And it was likely to change some more if he returned either of these calls. Why couldn't life just roll on smoothly without such up-sets? What would change if he called Jenny? Maybe he would say something that would mess up their friendship. But calling her back might help things work out. And with Toby, what if he gave the man bad advice? Toby was risking everything with this de-cision, after all.

Nodding checked the time on his watch. It was already nine-thirty. He needed to think about everything a little more. He made certain the doors were locked before he headed to bed.

The next morning was cloudy. Nodding noticed a few snow-flakes blowing by the window, but the weatherman promised it wouldn't accumulate. Saturday was supposed to be cold and sunny, and he thought about asking Jenny to have dinner with him then. He decided to wear a heavy sweater because it looked windy outside, then left for work.

The morning was quiet. He planned menu choices for a month ahead, then caught himself looking at the desk telephone. Finally he picked it up and called Toby, but his wife Jean said he was at church and always left his phone at home. She told him they were excited about summer on the South Shore. He said he hoped to meet her soon and would call Toby later.

"You hear about these new studies?" Kwasi said as he came into the office with a food service magazine. "One of them came out of Dal."

"Caffeine?" Nodding said, reaching for his coffee mug. "They want to ban it from pop. I don't see how they make the argument stick. And look at gourmet coffee drinks. Ten years ago no trucker in his right mind would ask for an amaretto blend at a truck stop, but these guys today order it as often as regular."

"This other study says moderate alcohol use can help fight heart disease," Kwasi said. "That's one to three drinks a day. So is it healthier to have a beer with your cereal instead of coffee?"

"Your kidneys and liver would know the difference. But maybe a beer with your steak would help counteract the fat and cholesterol."

"I guess I'll go eat a doughnut on my break," Kwasi said. "At least everyone agrees they're no good for you."

He left and Nodding smiled. Small talk was Kwasi's way of touching base, seeing how Nodding was doing without intruding. Before long Kwasi would be gone from the cafeteria, making big dollars as a manager or executive. He had a bright future.

Nodding went back to his paperwork until lunch time. He thought he would beat Jenny to the corner table, but she was already there with a burger when he came out of the office.

"You look great," he said as he sat down across from her. One cheek was swollen a bit, but she had covered the bruise with makeup.

"I'm still tired, but I feel okay," she said. "One day and I got sick of hospital food. Aren't you going to eat?"

"I'll grab a bite later. You all settled at Audrey's?"

"It's nice. She's got like a million pictures all over the walls of her relatives and friends. It made me realize I don't have any, not even of my parents. I think I oughta call them or something."

"I bet they miss you a lot."

"I doubt it," she said. "By the time I left they were pretty sick of our fights and all. They never did like Conrad."

She was wearing a grey turtleneck sweater and loose black pants, and Nodding noticed the ring was still on her finger.

"You feel up to having dinner tomorrow night?" he said. "We could go somewhere nice to celebrate you getting out of the hospital."

"Yeah," she said, her eyes meeting his. "But you have to let me pay for my half. You've already been through enough on account of me, and I don't want you going broke or anything."

"I can afford a meal or two. You can pay for me next time, if you want to."

"Okay," she said. "I better get back and relieve Audrey. She did all my work while I was away, so I'd feel guilty if I'm late today."

"She wanted to do it," Nodding said.

"Well, I guess. You two have done so much for me. I really appreciate it."

She reached over and squeezed his hand, then stood up slowly. "I get stiff if I sit too long."

Nodding took her tray and walked her to the door. After she left, he dropped her dishes at the counter, then got himself a bowl of tomato soup and went back to the table.

Audrey Katz showed up a few minutes later with a sandwich. "That girl eats like a bird," she said. "I made a meatloaf with cheese chunks last night, and she only had a piece and a little nibble for seconds."

"She looks good," Nodding said.

"We went over to her apartment. She filled a suitcase with clothes and a policeman stayed there with us. It was just so depressing, David. There were no pictures on the walls or anything. It was like a motel room, except the furniture looked like it came from a thrift shop."

"I asked her to have dinner with me tomorrow," he said.

"Did she say yes?"

He nodded.

"That's just grand. Take her someplace romantic, David. That Conrad probably never took her anywhere nice."

"I'll have to think about where to go."

"I'm relieved you're taking her," Audrey said. "I usually spend Saturday evenings with my friend Alberta. We catch an early dinner and then go to the firehall and play bingo. I know she'd miss it if I cancelled, but Jenny shouldn't be alone."

"I'll be by about five," he said.

He finished his soup and she folded up her napkin.

"I probably shouldn't say a word, but I can't resist." Audrey leaned across the table. "She has a tattoo, David. It's cute, really, but not small. At her age I would have never given it a thought, but I guess these days it's the rage."

"Where is it?"

"Never you mind, and don't you say a word or she'll know I told you." Audrey patted his shoulder on her way out.

That evening, Nodding decided on the Bistro for dinner. It was small, in the centre of town, and a bit elegant. It would give them a chance to talk without having to drive far or wait for a table in one of the restaurants more popular with students. He called for a reservation, then ate dinner quickly and tidied up his townhouse.

It was still snowing off and on outside, so Nodding put a wax log in his fireplace and lit it. By eleven he had mopped the kitchen floor but wasn't tired. He turned on the late television news and waited through the weather.

It was still supposed to be nice through the weekend, so he turned off his television and went to bed. He had a dream about getting a tattoo on his chest that said 'JESUS SAVES.'

Saturday morning his doorbell rang just after he finished his cereal. Nodding expected it to be Mrs. Saks, but found Toby on his doorstep.

"I needed to get out of the house for a while, and my pickup just came on down the highway," Toby said, shrugging off his coat. "I promise I won't keep you long, Dave."

"Don't worry," Nodding said. "I don't have anywhere I have to be."

He got Toby a mug of coffee, and they sat in the living room.

"I'm in a tight spot," Toby said. "Jean and the kids are just nuts to spend the summer in Port Medway. And I keep telling myself it's the right thing to do. I mean, I keep thinking of the Lord saying 'Come unto me all ye that labour and are heavy laden, and I will give you rest.' People can go to Hagan's hotel and rest their bodies and their souls."

"Then what's the matter?"

"I guess I'm scared. Jesus might have more faith in me than I do."

He took a swallow of coffee and put the mug down carefully. "This all sounds great, Dave, but I don't have the foggiest idea how to do that job. Everyone says I'm perfect for it, but I keep thinking what they'll say when I can't hack it."

"But you can do it," Nodding said. "I couldn't, Toby. Hagan

couldn't. But you know the kind of people the resort will attract. And you know the kinds of things they'll want to do in their free time. Just provide good clean fun for them, like you will for your family. Schedule worship services and maybe a discussion or two. If something works, do it again. If it doesn't, try something else."

"It's one thing talking about the Lord over the radio or in a truck stop. If they scoff or get rude, I can leave. I'm wondering now if I have the heart to stick it out. Won't be a truck waiting in the parking lot if things go wrong."

"I wish I had an answer," Nodding said. "But you have to decide for yourself."

"That is the answer," Toby said, standing up. "My problem is I was trying to think it through, when all along Jesus had offered me the path. It might be a test, working for a man like Hagan, but God wants me there. Like the good book says, He's leading me to the waters of comfort. Thank you, Dave. You've helped me through it all."

"I didn't do a thing. You'll have that hotel filled up before you know it."

"But we can't light up a 'NO VACANCY' sign, not ever. We always gotta have room at the inn, just in case."

"Keep a supply of cots," Nodding said. "Thanks for stopping by."

"You fed me coffee and listened to my troubles," Toby said, pulling on his coat. "Golly, I do wish you'd move down there, too. Maybe we could find you a nice young lady and get you settled and happy. Jean's a good matchmaker."

"I have a date tonight. Things are looking up."

"Well, God bless you, then."

Toby grabbed Nodding's hand. "Thanks again, Dave. I'll be in touch."

He opened the door and winked before he pulled it shut behind him.

Nodding picked up the coffee mugs and had just put them in the sink when his telephone rang,

16: Great evening

"David?" It was Mrs. Saks. "Could you come over for a minute?"

"Sure," he said. He didn't bother putting on a jacket, but hurried across the street.

She opened the door before he could knock. "Come in here before you freeze to death. Can I make you a cup of tea or hot chocolate? I have some instant coffee."

"I'm fine," Nodding said. He followed her into the living room and sat beside her on the couch.

"That Mr. Mayoubi called me last night."

"Wissam? Are you certain?"

"Who else could it be? The telephone rang at almost midnight and when I answered, he didn't say a word. My phone said it was from a 'private caller'. Isn't that just like him? Anyway, I was half asleep, so I just hung up. I told you he'd be back."

"Maybe it was Conrad, the guy with the gun."

"No, he's just a hooligan. But that Mr. Mayoubi is rotten to the core. I took that rug he left for me and put it in the dumpster. I suspect it had heroin dust or nerve poison on it."

She wiped her hands on her skirt. "Are you sure I can't get you something to drink, dear?"

"I'm fine," Nodding said. "Did you call the police?"

"No, they're convinced he's long gone." She shook her head. "That's why I called you, David. I'm going on a little trip until this business calms down. I'm just an old lady and no match for a band of terrorists."

"Where are you going? A vacation will be good for you."

"I told my friend Dolores I was heading for Cuba next Thursday, She'll be stopping by every now and then to water my plants. She drives a red Ford, you know."

"I'll watch for it," he said.

"I'm sorry I didn't have a chance to meet that poor dear in the hospital," she said. "You keep an eye on her now, David."

She stood up to see him to the door.

"I will. Send me a card from Cuba. I'll think of you whenever it snows."

"Keep your eyes peeled,"she said, looking out her peephole before opening the door. "You can't trust a living soul."

"Have a great time," Nodding said, heading out onto her front steps.

"I'll be too busy to have any fun. You keep an eye on things here for me."

"Well, enjoy Cuba," he said, heading down her steps.

"Hush, I'm not going there. I'm going undercover. Now, mum's the word."

"Wait," Nodding said, stopping. "Where are you going? What are you up to?"

"You'll hear from me, David. Until then, just act normal."

The door shut and Nodding stood for a moment staring at the peephole, wondering if she was watching. After a minute he went home.

He called the Bistro later that morning and requested a table near the fireplace. By three he was in the shower, and then he sat until four-thirty watching hockey on television. The game was pretty dull, and it was only when he stood up to turn off the television that he realized he didn't know which teams were playing.

He chose a tie that went with his shirt and knotted it carefully.

He drove over to the supermarket and bought a bouquet of carnations, which looked much fresher than the roses. Then he drove through town to Audrey's apartment building, just down from the Coastal Inn.

Jenny was waiting in the parking lot. She opened the door and hopped in before he could get out to greet her.

"Here," he said, handing her the flowers. "I thought these might cheer you up a bit."

"They're beautiful. Damn, are pants and a sweater okay? You're all dressed up."

"You look great. This place is informal," *Which is true*, he thought, and wondered why he'd worried himself into a coat and tie.

Jenny was wearing tight blue slacks and a white sweater, from what he could see through her open coat.

They were quiet on the short drive. Jenny looked at the flowers, then out the window.

"This is the first time anyone's ever given me flowers," she said. "I mean, it seems like such a simple thing, but no one ever did."

"I would have gotten roses, if I'd known."

"Ah, you shouldn't have even gotten me these, David. But thanks."

"Did you get some rest today?"

"I slept late," she said. "Audrey snuck around all morning, so she wouldn't wake me up. It was funny, because the floor in front of the bedroom squeaks, so every time she went by I could hear her. She kept making 'shhh' sounds at the floor."

"You look healthier than you did yesterday."

She was quiet then, until Nodding parked near the restaurant. He tried to hurry around the car to help her out, but she was quick and got out before he could get there.

"Will you relax?" Jenny said. "It's not like I'm some high school date you have to be polite to, you know. I'm the one who got her hand stuck in the candy machine. Remember?"

"How could I forget?" he said, managing to hold the door for her as they went in.

They sat at a table in front of the fireplace and enjoyed the warmth and crackling glow while they looked over the menu. Their waiter took their drink orders, and Jenny asked for a glass of white wine. Nodding remembered the alcohol study and ordered a Lunenburg Stout.

"I've never tried one of those," Jenny said. "Conrad always drinks Bud Light. He says it's as good as any other."

"Any kind of Stout is a little different."

"I didn't take any of my pain pills today," she said. "I wanted to have some wine with dinner and I was afraid I'd pass out if I had a pill, too."

"Just about everything here is good," Nodding said. "The seafood is right off the boats."

"What are you having?" she said.

"I'm celebrating. I think I'll have scallops."

"I like those, but I think I'll have salmon. One thing I will never eat is snails. They look so slimy."

"They taste like garlic to me. I tried them once, and that was enough."

"Out west where my cousins live they eat about everything," Jenny said. "When I was a kid we went to see them and I ate rabbit and squirrel. They said muskrat tastes good, but I never tried it."

"Venison is good," Nodding said. "But I don't think I ever want to try muskrat. Just the name is enough to turn me off."

The waiter came and took their order. They decided to share a plate of crabcakes as an appetizer, and when they came they were hot and spicy. Nodding ordered another beer, but Jenny sipped her wine and said she was fine for now.

The fire seemed to be getting warmer, so Nodding slipped off his jacket and felt better. Jenny said she was fine, but her face seemed a bit flushed.

"I'm sorry I asked for a table next to the fire," he said. "I thought it would be nice, but I didn't think about it being too hot."

"It's fine. I always want our mobile a lot warmer than Conrad. I guess maybe I have cold blood or something."

The waiter arrived with their meals and Jenny said her salmon was delicious.

"What are you going to do about your apartment?" Nodding said. His scallops were lightly seared, just as he would have prepared them.

"I already called. I'm moving my things out on Monday, and an auctioneer is taking the furniture during the week. Most of it is junk, anyway." She used her knife to push a last nibble of salmon onto her fork.

"Won't you need your furniture for a new place?"

"David, I can't stay around here," Jenny said. "If I do, Conrad will hang around and get arrested. He could go to jail right now if they arrest him, and then I don't know what I'd do."

"You wouldn't end up in the hospital."

"Yeah, I know. My feelings are all over the place."

She put down her fork. "Here I am, getting us all depressed. I don't want to mess up this dinner. Are the scallops good?"

"Very tender. I'm glad the salmon was good."

"It was delicious." She took a last sip of her wine. "I don't think Conrad meant to hurt me that bad, really. He just got carried away."

"It wasn't the first time he hit you. And it won't be the last."

"I don't know. Maybe I'm not thinking right. But you and Audrey don't really know him, David. Sure, he has a mean side, but he has a real good side, too. That's the side I see most of the time. That's the side that loves me."

"I don't believe anyone who loves someone would hurt them. Ever," Nodding said. He had planned on dessert, but he suddenly had no appetite.

"David, you're different. You're a lot more grown up and calm than Conrad. He's like a little kid inside, all confused and hurt. He can't control those feelings sometimes, but underneath it all, he's really sweet."

"All I can go on is what I've seen. He was shooting a gun at an innocent guy."

"I know. And even then you've been wonderful to me, even bringing me flowers."

"I like you," he said.

"I know that."

She reached over and took his hand, which had been clenching his napkin. "I don't want to hurt you, David. I know you feel attracted to me, and you're so kind to me, but I realized in the hospital that, deep down, I still really love Conrad."

"How can you? He treats you like a dog. You're too good for that, Jenny."

She looked down at her plate and blinked her eyes. She shook her head.

"You are," he said.

"I wanted this to be such a nice evening. I'm sorry. I shouldn't have said any of this until later. It all just came out once I started talking. I'm sorry."

"This is as good a time as any."

"You don't really know me, David," she said. "I think I kind of led you on before, and I'm sorry. It was just so nice having a guy for a friend, you know? And I still want to be your friend, even if we can't see each other much."

"What are you going to do?"

He let go of her hand. He wiped his face and put his napkin back in his lap. The fire seemed even hotter.

"We're going west. Conrad says there are lots of jobs in Alberta, and it's cheap to live there." She arranged her knife and fork on her plate.

The waiter appeared and began taking away their plates. "Any dessert for you folks, or coffee? We have our secret-recipe peanut butter pie tonight."

"I can't hold another bite," Jenny said. Nodding shook his head, and the waiter went away.

"I mean it David. I am so sorry. I wouldn't hurt you for anything.",

"I'm okay," Nodding said. Then: "You've seen him since he hurt you!"

"He came to the hospital just before I got out. He brought me some candy, chocolate with cherries inside. He was so upset, David. He even cried and begged me not to leave him."

The waiter brought the bill and Nodding dug into his wallet.

"I know I've upset you, David. That's one reason I'm leaving with him, because it wouldn't be fair to stay around and not talk to you. I told Conrad you were a friend like Audrey and he believes me. He said he hasn't slept for days because he's worried about me."

"Just be careful," Nodding said. "If he ever hurts you again, you can call me."

"He won't," Jenny said. "It scared him when he beat me up."

"Promise me you'll get help when he hits you again."

"I will. I'll be fine, really." Her tears had washed away a bit of her makeup, and Nodding could see little stripes of bruise on her left cheek.

The waiter brought the change and Nodding sorted out a good tip.

"I want to pitch in," Jenny said.

"Save your money," Nodding said. He managed a smile. "You'll probably need it."

They put on their coats and went out to the parking lot.

"It's getting colder," Jenny said. "But at least it's clear."

Nodding unlocked her door and held it for her, then climbed in on his side.

"When are you leaving?" he said. He started the engine and looked over at her.

"Tuesday. I made him wait until I had a chance to thank you and clear the apartment. He understood."

"What about Audrey?"

"I told her before she left for bingo. I made her promise not to call the police. She thinks I'm crazy."

"So do I," Nodding said.

They drove back in the cold without saying anything.

When they got to Audrey's building, Jenny leaned over and kissed Nodding's cheek. "You're a wonderful guy, David. Thanks again."

"Call me if you need anything," he said, watching as she climbed out. "Take care of yourself."

"Bye." She turned and went into the building.

"Great evening," he said to the car.

He watched until Jenny was inside, then drove out of the parking lot and headed home. "Here I go again," he said. "I'll sit around and mope and be alone just like before. Why'd I even get involved in the first place? Maybe I should just play bingo with Audrey and her friend."

He parked in front of his steps and saw Mrs. Saks had her lights out. He opened his front door and surveyed his living room. It was warm and comfortable, but tonight it felt lonely.

Nodding sat down and stared at the television for about fifteen minutes. Then he got up and went into the kitchen, but he was still full from dinner.

On the way back to his chair he pulled out his cell phone. He looked up the number and called, but no one answered, so he left a message.

"Toby," he said, "I need Hagan's number. I've changed my mind."

17: Promised land

Nodding drove to Port Medway the next weekend to talk with Hagan. They agreed to meet at HAGAN'S HAVEN at ten o'clock on Saturday morning, so Nodding left work at noon on Friday. This would allow time if the highway was icy, but it was clear.

He didn't tell anyone at work where he was going or why, just in case the hotel was a dump and he re-changed his mind.

"I just might meet you boys down there," Toby had said. "We could get our pictures taken tearing down the NO VACANCY sign, just to let Jesus know we're serious."

Nodding only hoped there was such a sign and that it was occasionally needed.

The drive was smooth, taking him through Truro, then up the hill where he and Toby had crashed. From there, the highway crossed rural farm lands populated with frequent gas stations and occasional motels. When he turned onto the 103, the land grew more rugged. Crews were "twinning" the highway, and Nodding was impressed with how many huge boulders lined the road.

But the highway narrowed before Bridgewater, where he planned to spend the night. After this the big box stores would be left behind. Other than expensive ocean resorts, motels would be rare until Liverpool, south of the Port Medway turnoff.

Nodding got off the highway and checked into the Best Western for the night. He ate an early dinner next door at the Boston Pizza, enjoying their tasty spaghetti and meatballs. Then, feeling satisfied, he walked back to his room and went to bed.

Saturday morning, Nodding was up early and excited about the day ahead. He checked out, then drove back into Bridgewater. He parked at the Esso station and went inside. Behind the usual soda and snack shop he found Jerry's Diner, which Kwasi had urged him to visit. There he ate a solid South Shore breakfast, complete with baked beans and lots of coffee.

He asked his waitress how long it would take to drive to Port Medway and she laughed.

"Half an hour on the highway," she said. "But the turnoff takes you back ten years. There's a bunch of artists lives there, plus an empty meeting house. No place to eat except the firehouse when they have some event, like twice a year. But we can pack you a hearty lunch, honey."

"Isn't there some resort there?"

"Oh yeah, big old place that packs them in by the busload in the summer. But they're all holy rollers, I hear. They stay on the property for the most part, though some sneak off to the only store in town to buy booze. Come winter, when the roads get greasy, the place is dead."

Nodding declined the offer of a box lunch, got back on the 103, heading south. He passed produce stands and gas stations, but generally he was surrounded by evergreen forest.

In half an hour he came to the Port Medway exit and turned left. He drove along the quiet road for about ten minutes, seeing some plowed driveways but not much else.

Not much changed when he entered the village. Gradually there were more homes along the road, older and well maintained.

At the one main intersection, he paused. Ahead were the lighthouse and boat yard, so he turned right. He passed the fire department and meetinghouse. After a bit he could see the water on his left, and then he came to the hotel and a plowed driveway.

The original hotel was three stories tall, built in 1946, and set back a bit from the ocean for protection from bad weather. Cheap post-war labour had allowed Hagan's grandfather to sink a concrete wall into the sand, which had protected the hotel during several major storms. It wasn't visible now, Hagan had said. But under the sand it was still there, waiting as climate change threatened.

Nodding noticed that even the lightning rods were painted white, and he smiled to see the tallest, on a chimney, was bent to form a halo shape.

Hagan's parents had taken over the property in 1968, building a forty-unit motel closer to the highway. In 1990, after Hagan's father died, his mother had converted the hotel to a religious retreat, adding a chapel and meeting rooms to the complex.

Nodding passed the entrance, slowing to look in. The buildings looked to be in good repair. The main hotel was wooden, painted white. The motel unit and chapel were brick, also painted white. The parking lot was gravel, and only a small sign on the highway identified the resort.

He felt himself relax a bit. It looked like a well-kept piece of property.

Just beyond the chapel was a white frame house, which would be Toby's. It was empty and dark as Nodding passed.

Nodding continued down Long Cove Road for about ten minutes until he came to the Medway Head lighthouse and the open ocean. He turned around and drove back to the hotel without seeing any other travellers.

He turned into the resort and saw an older white pickup truck parked by the main building, next to a blue Mustang. He wondered which was Hagan's as he walked to the door. A bumper sticker on the truck read SHIT HAPPENS, and now he knew.

"See? Right on the button." Hagan was sitting in the lobby in his parka, talking to a slender black man with white hair who was in a chair next to him. The lights were on, but the lobby was cold.

"Dave, come over and meet Moses Tanner." They both stood up.

"Dave Nodding," he said, shaking hands. He could see his breath in the room, and then he saw that Hagan's face was swollen.

"Are you okay?"

"Dentist. My old woman sent me out to get my teeth cleaned yesterday, and damned if he didn't fill two of them suckers and yank one clean out. Hurts like hell when I try to chew my dip."

"Your mother didn't allow chewing tobacco," Moses said. "Too many people dripped on the carpet."

"Well, I ain't a guest and I won't drip," Hagan said. "And I can't chew anything today, so don't worry."

"Want me to turn up the heat?" Moses said. "We keep the up-stairs zone at forty five because of the plumbing, but the lobby feels colder."

"Can you heat up the office?" Hagan said. "Dave might like to peek over the books and all."

"Right away." Moses left the lobby at a brisk pace.

"That's one guy we gotta keep happy," Hagan said. "He's honest, he's smart, and he knows every inch of this place."

"Has he worked here long?"

"They came here a few years after my Pa died. His wife, Virginia, she's head of the cleaning staff. Two of their daughters work here in the summer. They have a third, but Moses told me she married a guest two years ago and moved to Cheticamp."

"Can I explore a bit?" Nodding said.

"Let Moses show you the place first," Hagan said. "You can get to know him a little, and he knows the kind of stuff you'll want to see. I'm goin' into the office and take some pills for this mouth. Jesus, it hurts."

"Don't blame Him, but ask Him to heal your pain, brother." Toby stood in the door, beaming. "Ain't this a glorious day?"

"Hey, Preacher, you're in time for the tour. I'm taking a toothache break."

"I believe a toothache is a reminder of life in Hell," Toby said. "Just think of Jesus as the Novocaine of life." He walked over and shook Hagan's hand.

"I don't know," Hagan said. "Nothing hurt until I went to the dentist. And his Novocaine wore off last night."

"Good to see you again, Dave," Toby said. "I can't tell you how my day lit up when I heard you was coming down. Praise God for life's blessings."

"Praise the painkillers," Hagan said. "My mouth is on fire here." As he left the lobby, he said, "I'll send Moses to show you guys around."

"I already talked to Hagan about the name," Toby said. "HAGAN'S HAVEN doesn't sound too spiritual. Sounds to me like a campground."

"Have any ideas?" Nodding said, looking around the lobby.

It was clean, with wide wooden flooring and sturdy wicker furniture, a space designed for summer, with large ceiling fans in place. On the wall behind the front desk was a large print of da Vinci's *The Last Supper*.

"Yeah, but my wife said no." Toby stuck his hands in his pockets and looked at his boots. "I thought of 'The Bethlehem Inn', but Jean said it was too showy. I said we could call it 'The Stables', but she laughed at me. Said we'd only get a few horses stopping by, and I guess she was right."

"But Hagan agreed to change the name?"

"Oh yeah. He meant what he said, Dave. He wants us to run this place, and he'll do what we suggest. He won't interfere. But he wants us to save the old sign."

"I guess it has sentimental value," Nodding said.

Moses came into the lobby, holding two cups of coffee.

"He has this plan," Toby said. "I'll tell you later."

"Thought you gents would like to start with the main show," Moses said. "It's why they all come here, and why they come back."

"The chapel?" Toby said.

"No, I had the beach in mind. This original building has the dining room on the second floor, with a big porch around the back. There's even a little boardwalk out to the gazebo, where some of the older folks go to take the air."

He nodded at the wide stairway and started up. "Right this way."

"Hagan told me there was an elevator, too," Toby said, carrying his coffee carefully. "I guess a number of the guests are older."

"We get all ages," Moses said. "The elevator is down the hall from the desk, near the office. Mrs. Hagan had it put in just after her husband passed."

"Look at this," Nodding said at the top of the stairs.

Ahead of them was the dining room, with huge windows facing the beach and water. Every table in the large, high-ceilinged room had a view. There were no booths, but only tables for four that could be arranged as desired.

"Would you look at that bright blue water," Toby said. "Probably a bit cold for a swim today."

"I'll let you gents stroll out to the gazebo," Moses said, leading them to a door at the edge of the dining room. "There's a much better view of the water from there, and you can also see how most of the rooms have an ocean view." He opened the door and stepped back.

"You aren't coming?" Toby said.

"Not in winter. This is as close as I get to that damn ocean air."

"Be back in a minute," Nodding said, heading out.

It seemed a bit warmer than earlier, but he realized the hotel had chilled him. In the gazebo, he took a sip of coffee and breathed in deeply. "This is amazing."

Beyond the gazebo the sand sloped softly to the gently lapping water.

"It's like God is talking just to us," Toby said. "It's a message, Dave."

"The beach? The water?" Nodding stopped and looked back. Toby had turned to look at the hotel. Moses saw them and gave a salute.

"Moses, Dave." Toby looked at Nodding, his eyes wide. "He led us up from below and to the water's edge. But he had to stop, just like in the good book. Can you believe it?"

"That is a little weird."

"It means we've made it, Dave."

Toby had tears in his eyes, and he put his coffee down on the gazebo railing so he could clasp his hands. "Thank you, Jesus, for giving us this chance."

"Amen," Nodding said. Moses was no longer in the doorway.

"You don't see yet, do you?" Toby said, coming over and pointing at the beach. "Moses didn't enter the promised land, but his people kept going. This is it, Dave. We're there. We've come home to serve the Lord."

He dropped to his knees in the gazebo, his arms reaching skyward.

Nodding gazed at the ocean. "Just look at this beach. It's like the old resorts in the movies. The beach is sheltered, so no big waves. It's just peaceful and uncrowded here."

"I'll pray here every morning," Toby said. "This beach will keep me on the path and living a righteous life."

He took a deep breath and looked at the hotel. "Moses is waiting."

Moses took them through the kitchen and pantries, then upstairs to the apartments on the third floor. The smallest would be Nodding's. It had a pleasant living room and bath, and a good-sized bedroom. He noted which furniture would fit.

None of the apartments had kitchens.

There were eight guestrooms at one end of the floor. Another four rooms were on the second floor, beyond the dining room and kitchen.

The motel units were fairly standard, but there were no televisions. Above each bed was the same painting of Jesus smiling down, arm raised in benediction. To Nodding's relief, none had a black velvet background. Each room had a telephone and clock radio. Nodding looked at the desks and found not only a Bible but a prayer book and hymnal in each.

The lower floor rooms looked out on the parking lot and dunes, but the water was an easy stroll away. The chapel and conference rooms were simple but nicely decorated, and Nodding returned to the lobby impressed.

"Have you lived in the area long?" he said.

"Just over fifteen years," Moses said. "After I got married, we left Halifax and came down here. But I'm from Zaire originally."

"How'd you end up in Halifax?"

"My brother was in the army at home, and he took me aside and said, 'The killing is coming soon.' He said America is the only safe country. But America is full of hatred toward Africans, so I came here instead. And you know, he was right. Even now Zaire is full of killing. You never know who's to be next."

"Is your brother still there?" Toby said.

"He's a general now," Moses said. "He tells me he is still scared every day. Killing never stops."

"It's happening everywhere," Nodding said,

"That is why we're here," Moses said. "Even Halifax and Dartmouth are violent now. I been here fifteen years, and I thought it was bad when I left. Judgment day is coming, It just has to be. Why else?"

"Port Medway is pretty quiet, compared to Halifax," Nodding said.

"Every town has problems. But here I don't worry about my wife or daughters walking outside. This is a good place to live and wait for the Lord."

"Do you think Toby and I could fit in here and keep this place running?"

"Oh yeah," Moses said, stopping at the front door. "Mr. Hagan, now, when I met him I was a little worried. Lots of the guests here wouldn't accept him right away. But I think you and Mr. Tobias understand what our guests are like. These aren't very wild people who stay here."

"We'll need a lot of help from you and everyone else," Nodding said. "Hagan said some people were quitting."

"Dollie left right after Mrs. Hagan passed away," Moses said. "But she was a mean-spirited and racist woman anyway. Virginia and I liked Mrs. Hagan, but no one here will leave just because Dollie did. African or indigenous folks had to step lightly around her."

He held the front door for them and they trooped back into the lobby.

"What do you think?" Hagan said. He was lying on a couch near the desk. "Looked okay when I went through, but what would I know?"

"It has real promise," Nodding said. "I'm impressed, so when you feel up to it, I'm ready to sit down and talk some business."

"I'm feeling better," Hagan said. "Let's go back to your future office. There's a heater there keeping it warm for us. We'll talk a bit and then I'll get the lawyers to put it all on paper for you this week."

"Great." Nodding turned to Moses. 'Thanks for the tour. I'm looking forward to working with you."

"Amen to that," Toby said. "I know now Jesus brought me to the right place."

"He led me here and gave me peace," Moses said. "It's a good place to live, here beside the water."

"Oughta call it The Still Waters," Hagan said. "Ain't that from the Bible?"

"God bless, there's hope for you yet," Toby said, looking at him. "Has a ring to it."

"Stillwaters?" Moses said. "That sounds peaceful and nice."

"I like it," Nodding said. He looked over at Toby and smiled.

"Let's order the sign, Moses," Hagan said. "Come on in, Dave, before my pill wears off."

He turned to look at Moses over his shoulder. "Save me that old sign, case I want to open a pub in Liverpool someday. Never can tell."

In the office they talked about responsibilities, and Hagan explained that Nodding would be in charge of the whole centre, with Toby working for him.

"He insisted," Hagan said. "That damn preacher has a way of making his point, too. Said it was God's will and who were we to tinker with it."

Hagan offered Nodding a raise in salary and the apartment year round, plus board when the hotel was open. He agreed to a two year contract. Nodding was thrilled, but managed to stay calm while they discussed the centre's annual budget and Nodding's fund for staff salaries. Hagan would handle salaries for Toby, Moses and Virginia at first, but Nodding would take care of the rest.

"We just finished my business here," Hagan said. "It feels damn weird talking money and not asking for it, you know? Things feel different from this side."

He stood up and offered his hand. "We're renting an apartment down near Liverpool. "So call me if I can help. The lawyers know to get you operating money for spring, but just call if you need more."

"You moving down here for good? Or just enjoying the summers?"

"Not sure yet. Only thing I'll miss up there is a good Chinese restaurant. So we're moving down here for now, until Lucille figures out where she wants to spend her winters."

"Anything I should know about the town or anyone in it?"

"Not much of a town. Grocery and food shop closed. Only other store sells booze. People are mostly good folks. Some of the old farts are too stuffy for me, but they was real good to my pa. They even tolerated my mother, which is more than I could do. Shit." He shook his head. "Damn."

"Tooth again?"

"No, it's my talking. Lucille says now I'm rich I gotta stop saying 'shit.' Hell, I been talking this way for more than thirty years. You can't just change something like that. And besides, I don't know what else to say. 'Fooey' just don't sound right coming out of my mouth."

"Guess that's life when you hang out with the rich guys," Nodding said.

"Don't tell the preacher," Hagan said. "He'll think I'm coming over to his way of thinking."

He dug into his pocket and handed Nodding a heavy keyring. "Moses can show you which opens what. I promised an old buddy I'd stop in for a chat, and shit, I'm running late."

He stopped for a second. "Hell with it, anyway."

In the lobby they met Toby and Moses and said goodbye to Hagan, who shook hands and then wandered out without looking back.

Nodding suggested they stop nearby for lunch on the way home and invited Moses to join them, but he shook his head and smiled.

"Virginia's got me on lettuce for lunch these days. I'll get the lights and heat before I go. We live down one of the drives coming into town. So let me know when you'll be back and I'll warm up units in the motel for you. No sense having to stay anywhere else."

"I'll come down next weekend," Nodding said. "Can we meet sometime after I go over the books and reservations folder? I'll need your advice on staffing for the summer."

"Call the hotel number and leave a message," Moses said. "I don't always have my cell turned on in winter. But I come in every day, and I'll bring Virginia in when you want to meet her."

18: Picture this

Toby and Nodding met at a restaurant on the highway north. Toby ordered meatloaf without potatoes, while Nodding had a turkey sandwich. The turkey was moist, but Nodding would have added a little less lettuce and a touch of Dijon mustard.

They chatted about the area a bit, and Nodding decided to drive down every weekend until he left work in late March. After that, he'd be in Port Medway full-time. He'd have two full weeks to prepare for the season opening, on Easter weekend in mid-April. Toby planned to move down himself about the same time, but his wife and kids would follow in July.

When he finished his meatloaf, he asked for a cup of coffee and a slice of apple pie. "I know the kids will make friends here. But finishing the school year is the most important thing for them."

"I still find it hard to believe Hagan trusts me as much as he does," Nodding said. "I gave him my supervisor's name with the food service, but he said he wouldn't call her."

"Dave, I've known Chester for eight years, and I have yet to really understand him. He sure don't follow the Christian path, but he's always been honest and friendly to me. He talks a wild streak, but I don't ever recall seeing him drink more than a beer or two, and he's faithful as all get out to his wife."

"What's she like?"

"Lucille? She's a large woman, very outgoing, and she sure does love to laugh. Always has a cigarette in her hand, unless she's sipping a lemonade. Can't say I know her too well. Jean and I didn't run in the same circles when Hagan drove for my freight line."

"Does he let you call him Chester? I never heard that before."

"He doesn't mind Chet. I throw in a Chester or two when I get tired of being called 'The Preacher.' But I will say he's a good man at heart. He's decided he can trust you, so he'll do it without hesitation. I declare, if he ever turns to Jesus, Hagan will be a true Christian soldier."

"Think it will ever happen?"

"The Lord works wonders," Toby said, wiping his mouth. He sat back and smiled. "And turning Hagan to Jesus would certainly take a wonder, don't you know?"

After lunch Toby left to explore local churches, while Nodding drove home. Most of what he needed was in the books and folders he'd brought from the office. He also had a brochure from the local tourism office so he could look up more information on the area if he needed it.

The weather was grey, but at least it wasn't snowing or sleeting for his drive. He got off the highway for gas next to the airport near Halifax, where he bought a scratch-off lottery ticket and won ten dollars. He took his money and got back on the road, smiling.

When he got home to his parking lot after dark, the Buick was gone, and there was no sign of Mrs. Saks.

On Monday, Nodding submitted his two-month notice, then called Kwasi into the office. He explained what he planned to do and told Kwasi he had recommended his promotion to manager.

"You're crazy!" Kwasi said. "The job you tried to throw at me? You took it? Have you lost your mind completely?"

"I need a change."

"So shave your head, man. Get a new tattoo. Buy a sports car. Do any of those bored white guy things, but damn, Nodding, don't ruin your life."

"I think it might be a good job after all. I'm kind of excited by it."

"You were excited by Audrey's tuna roast with sauce, too, until you tasted it." Kwasi couldn't sit down any longer. "Listen, Nodding. It's all that Porter girl's fault. You aren't thinking straight. Call the office back. Tell them you changed your mind. Wait a week and think things over here. This is serious, man."

"I took all weekend, Kwasi. I like working here, but I'm not happy with my life. Maybe the change will be what I need. The job looks fun, and I don't think it can really hurt my resume. But thanks for worrying."

"Damn," Kwasi backed up two steps and sat down again. "You really think they might promote me?" He couldn't help smiling.

"I think so. I said you were ready to be a manager in your last evaluation. But we'll have to see what they decide."

He saw Audrey sitting by herself at the corner table in the cafeteria. "Look. Take a stab at planning a week's menu. See how you do." He took out a blank form and handed it to Kwasi.

"This is my weak area," Kwasi said. "You know that."

"I call it the menu planning trap," Nodding said. "Enjoy it."

He smiled at Kwasi and went to talk to Audrey.

"David, I feel so guilty. I was too ashamed to even set foot in here last week, and today there are rumours you're quitting." She hadn't tasted her roast beef sandwich.

"None of it's your fault," Nodding said. "Don't worry about it." He sat down and looked at the sandwich. "Too rare?"

"Not at all. Actually, it looks sinful." She picked it up and took a large bite, nodding at him.

"I thought a lot last week about Jenny," he said. "If I hadn't just come back from Rachel's wedding, none of this would have happened. I would have known better, but I went and acted like I was in high school."

"This is scrumptious. But I'd add a little horseradish next time.

Let it bite back a little."

She smacked her lips and peeled back the bread to look at the meat. "I almost called the police to come and get Conrad when he picked her up."

"It would have just made her unhappy," he said. "I should have known better than to get involved."

"You would have been much better for her, David. I still think so. Are the office rumours true?"

"I'm leaving, but not right away. And once I'm gone, Kwasi will need some help with the recipes. Keep after him to try new ideas."

"Don't you worry," Audrey said. "I'm testing some curry recipes this week. I can't wait."

She took another bite of her sandwich, then managed to talk with a piece of bread crust stuck to her lower lip. "Where will you go?"

"Over to Port Medway. I'm managing a conference centre."

"I thought you might head west," she said, then swallowed. "You know."

"I won't ever see her again," Nodding said. "I'm doing something completely new, and I won't have time to worry about Jenny and Conrad."

"I guess it's for the best. When will you be leaving?"

"The end of March. But I'll be spending weekends there until then."

"Well, that gives us two months to check out recipes for you to take along." She stood up.

"I'll take your tray, Audrey."

"Thanks for not being mad," she said. "Even if I am to blame."

"Get to work on the curry," Nodding said.

Once she was gone, he took her tray to the dish room, then went to warn Kwasi.

Later that afternoon Kwasi got a call from the office and was offered the promotion. He hurried to the office to see Nodding, who stood up, shook hands, and said, "Welcome to the Office Trap."

That night Nodding heated up a casserole and watched the news while he ate. During a break he got up to get more casserole, and on his way to his seat he peeked out the window. The parking lot was dark, the house next door still empty.

When he sat down again, Nodding realized there was no one else to tell he was leaving. Not much for a couple of years in Antigonish. The town had been such a welcome escape when he first came here, but he'd never settled in.

He looked around his living room, and it seemed as stark and sterile as a motel room.

He'd miss Mrs. Saks, but he'd leave his address with her friend. Maybe she'd even be back before he moved. Yesterday, driving home, he'd wondered about the move. Today, thinking it through again, he realized he could hardly wait.

On Valentine's Day Nodding was sorting through invoices at his desk when there was a knock on the door. He glanced up to see Detective Martin wiping snow out of his hair and smiling.

"Come in," Nodding said. "Can I get you a cup of coffee?"

"I'd love it. A little cream, no sugar. Thanks." He came into the office and settled into a chair.

Nodding hurried out, poured a mug, and brought it in.

"I hate this weather," Martin said. "I transferred here from Calgary to escape winter, but every once in a while it catches me."

"At least we're better off than Cape Breton," Nodding said.

"Got good news. Came in this morning. They picked up Mabou Conrad over in Hamilton, Ontario yesterday."

"What happens now?" He watched Martin sip his coffee and smack his lips.

"Normally, we'd get him up here for trial. but that little rascal did something stupid, so he's not going anywhere for awhile."

"What happened?"

"Picture this." Martin put down his coffee and leaned forward. "He's eating in some diner and goes outside to buy a paper. Puts in his money, or so he says, but the machine won't open. Now you or me, we might smack the machine a time or two. Not Conrad, He goes to his car, comes back with a gas can, and splashes gas over the newspaper machine. At least he was smart enough to let it evaporate a little, else he would have blown himself up. But then the guy tosses a match on it. Not too subtle. Two town cops were eating in the damned diner when he did it."

"And they arrested him," Nodding said.

"Tried. Conrad makes dumb mistake number two. He punches out the first cop to reach him, then kicks him when he falls over. The second officer weighs three hundred pounds and beat the living shit out of poor Mabou.

"So they won't be sending him back here."

"You got it. Once they unwire his jaw and get him into a courtroom, he's facing some vacation time in prison before we even have a crack at him. That young man has only begun to experience life, let me tell you." He rubbed his hands.

"Thanks for letting me know," Nodding said.

"No need to worry about him for a long time. Now, if I could get ahold of that Mayoubi guy, we could close this case for good."

"No sign yet?"

"He's slippery. But we got all of his buddies. Here we went and called immigration to trace him and damned if the whole family wasn't from Toronto. Total bunch of con men. But our man Mayoubi has bigger problems. My guess is we'll never hear another word about him."

"Why not?"

"The people he was selling the explosives to paid him off and ended up losing some big bucks. From what I hear, it's nearly half a million, and he's vanished with the money. These boys play for keeps. They're looking for Mayoubi a lot harder than I am. So if I had to guess, I'd say he was on a beach in Aruba, thinking he's safe."

"But he's not?"

"Not for half a million. No way." He stood up. "Anyway, I thought I should stop by and bring you up to date, At least you know Conrad won't be shooting at you. Thanks for the coffee." They shook hands and Martin pulled out a scarf.

"It'll warm up soon," Nodding said, watching him pull on a pair of gloves.

"I hate ice. Except on a rink." He waved as he went out.

Nodding glanced at his watch. Audrey would have already eaten lunch. He sat for a minute, then headed up to tell her the news, just in case Jenny called.

Friday evening Nodding drove to Port Medway for his third visit. He had spent the last weekend going over the books, happy to discover that Beulah Hagan had made a tidy profit the year before. With the budget Hagan had given him, he could make some improvements in the menu and upgrade aging bedding in some of the rooms. Meals were included in the rates package, which removed some uncertainty in the food budgeting

Nodding decided to monitor the first season closely to support a study of the food operation's effectiveness. It might pay to change the package system in future years if the food remained consistently good and if the customers weren't picky eaters. Recent menu records pointed at a meat and potatoes crowd as opposed to fine dining visitors.

Nodding had also discovered that the reservations system had been upgraded recently, allowing him to check availability instantly. By the end of the weekend he had programmed in new rates and explained the increases to Moses, who confessed he knew very little about the rooming operation. He promised to have Virginia come in the following weekend to talk it over with Nodding.

"She always took her break in with Mrs. Hagan," Moses said. "When things were busy, Virginia had to handle reservations now and again. She knows how it all works."

Nodding found a unit in the motel wing warm and unlocked when he arrived. The week's mail was on the desk in the room, as well as a note telling him Virginia would meet him at ten the next morning.

There were two written reservation requests, which made him a little nervous. He had played with the system, but now he'd have to mean business.

The next morning Nodding was up and ready early. He had stopped at the Bridgewater Timmy's the night before, getting a box of doughnuts and a couple of breakfast sandwiches to go. He took them over to the office in the hotel and made coffee while a sandwich heated in a microwave. The office was warm and the computer was turned on, so he knew he was not the first to arrive.

"Mr. Nodding? Good morning." He turned and smiled at a short, slender woman in the doorway. She was holding a coffee pot from the dining room. "If you're gonna be working in here with the cold, you'll need more than a cup from that capsule machine."

She looked about sixty, but it was hard to tell because there was no grey in her hair at all. She put down the coffee pot and shook his hand.

"It's nice to finally meet you," Nodding said. "Moses mentions you every time I see him, and I've been looking forward to seeing you myself."

"Moses talks about everyone and everything," Virginia said. "But he doesn't ever lie. I can put up with his jabbering, as long as it's honest."

I brought some doughnuts. Please help yourself."

"Oh, Boston Creme. Delicious, if you ain't fat or old like me. I don't let Moses eat fat any more, because of his blood pressure. I won't eat treats myself these days, except on special occasions."

"This is a special occasion," Nodding said. "I can't eat them all."

"You're a rascal," she said, smiling. "Not right now, but thank you."

She pointed at the computer screen. "Want me to show you the reservations?"

"Please," he said, and they pulled chairs up to the desk.

Virginia was no expert at keyboarding, but she understood how the program worked and explained it simply and clearly. Within twenty minutes Nodding understood how to create reports, search for specific data, and enter room requests.

"Want to switch from housekeeping to the office?" he said finally.

"No way, if it's up to me," Virginia said. "I'm one of those people, I just like to clean. If I stayed home, I'd be cleaning there. So I'd rather keep cleaning, if I have the choice."

"You do. Hagan said you should do whatever you want and I shouldn't get in your way. So if you like housekeeping, you're in charge of housekeeping."

"He's a good man. Bit wild, but that's 'cause his mama tried to push him too hard. Everybody told her to lay off, but she wouldn't listen."

"Moses said you two have lived here for fifteen years." Nodding poured himself more coffee from the pot.

"Little bit more," she said. "Come down here after we married to get a fresh start. I grew up in the city, got married, had kids, and lost my husband without ever seeing the province. Moses brought me down to Shelburne on our honeymoon, and I said 'We're moving,' and we did."

"So you have three daughters?"

"Oh, yeah. All good girls. One got married, the other two are still at home for now. They're all from my first husband.'

"You and Moses never had kids?"

"Moses won't," Virginia said. "Thinks the world is too violent to last. So it's just us, but he's like a father to my girls. They were all little when my husband died. I'll always remember, because he'd sit up nights in our apartment, watching the news and talking back to the television. I'd say 'Max, come to bed,' but he'd just sit there, like he was glued. Then one night I woke up and found him dead in his chair, Keith's half drunk and the tv still on."

She turned the computer off and stood up. "You can turn it on and practice some more, but I'm inspecting the rooms today. You just yell if you get stuck."

"I will," he said. "Thanks for making the coffee."

"You know one reason I like working here?" she said, pulling on a heavy cloth overcoat. "No television. I don't watch the news at home. People need to escape that stuff when they can."

She glanced at the computer. "I can't watch news any more without seeing Max dead in his chair. Me, I want to go thinking good thoughts."

She shook her head, then looked up. "Moses, he watches it."

"How far away do you all live? Nodding asked.

"Head out towards the 103," she said. "Sharp bend to the left, big pine, the next drive is us. Fifteen minutes. Pretty all year, and in summer heat a fan keeps us cool." She waved and went off to check rooms.

Nodding took the mailed reservation requests, entered them, then printed reports to see how they worked. It was far easier than he had feared, and he felt himself relaxing. He reached for a dough-nut while the printer finished his reports.

Before Virginia left, she showed him the laundry room, where staff handled kitchen towels and napkins. A Liverpool linen service took care of sheets and guest towels. Virginia explained they had switched over five years ago to save water and money, and found the service did a better job as well.

She explained housekeeping duties and mentioned they would need one new housekeeper for the summer. One of last year's was expecting a baby in June, so she had resigned. Virginia had a lead, so Nodding told her to hire a replacement she trusted.

"It's your department," he said. "Hire someone you want."

19: Didn't recognize you

Nodding spent the next few weekends familiarizing himself with the centre's operations. He went through the kitchen's menus and contacted the established suppliers. He changed the dairy the centre worked with to save money and speed deliveries, and the word must have gotten around.

Within a week sales calls were coming in, and established suppliers were far more eager to be helpful. Few sales people had liked Dollie, who had run the food operation. They were delighted to have a new contact.

Nodding sorted through employment applications and discovered that he'd need two new waiters and a desk clerk to complete the summer staff. He called area newspapers to place help-wanted ads, as well as putting notices on the STILLWATERS website. He met Toby for meals when both were down, and helped him arrange furniture in one of the apartments.

Moses wanted to paint the house before Toby moved in. Hagan's mother had left it furnished, so Toby's furniture would stay in his house up north until after the summer.

Nodding also took time to visit his apartment and make some plans. As he packed his Antigonish townhouse, he kept his new home in mind, so he had to leave behind many old books and university possessions. One lamp that he'd made in high school had sentimental value, but he even parted with that.

Nodding's actual move to Port Medway went smoothly. He said

goodbye to Kwasi and Audrey on his last day, when Kwasi held a small farewell gathering. Audrey promised to visit sometime, and Kwasi urged him to come to his senses one last time.

The next day, April Fool's Day, Toby showed up at dawn with a rented truck. They had Nodding's belongings loaded in two hours flat. They stopped for breakfast at the truckstop near Truro where they had met and then were on the road, with Nodding following the truck.

Moses and two friends were waiting in Port Medway to help unload. Even with the elevator, the extra muscles helped with his dresser, couch, desk, and bed.

Just as they finished, the chicken dinner Nodding had ordered from Dixie Lee's in Liverpool arrived. Virginia warmed it in a microwave, then everyone enjoyed fried chicken, poutine, and iced tea or pop in the dining room.

After Nodding had thanked everyone, he was alone to unpack and plan his future. He set up his bedroom first and went to bed with the window open a crack so he could listen to the welcome splashing of waves.

During the next week Nodding settled into his apartment and office. He got a small microwave so he could make a cup of coffee or heat up a snack late at night. He arranged his desk so he could sit and look out at the beach, which still looked wintry.

Two days after he moved in, the STILLWATERS sign arrived, and Moses supervised its installation. The company also brought a small blue neon star, which Toby had ordered for the roof on the ocean gazebo.

Nodding and Moses examined it while the sign workers were hanging the main sign. "Don't know about this one," Moses said. "Least he changed his mind from that JESUS SAVES thing he was looking at."

"Toby said the star will look good from the beach," Nodding said.

"It will shine out to sea, so you won't see it from the hotel."

"You know what I like?" Moses said. "Christmas time about five years ago, Mrs. Hagan took little white lights and strung them inside the gazebo and around the outside of its roof. It lit up the place real gentle, and I told her it looked mighty pretty. But come summer she took them down and had me plug in that big LED bulb. Said it would last longer and brighten up the area around the gazebo. I don't think many people sit out there at night anymore. A plain old light bulb would be easier on the eyes."

"Can we get some of those Christmas lights?" Nodding said,

"I kept them. Over in the storage garage by the house. I can get them hooked up and you can see them tomorrow night."

"Let's do it. I think it sounds great. Let's keep the smaller lights along the walkway the way they are, though, so none of the guests trip or fall. They aren't as bright as the LED."

"Good as done," Moses said.

"If you think of anything else that would improve how the place looks, let me know," Nodding said.

He noticed the old HAGAN'S HAVEN sign was loaded on the truck. "Didn't Hagan want to save that one?"

"They're taking it over to him," Moses said. "Hanging it over there."

"At his apartment?"

"I knew I hadn't been telling you enough," Moses said. "Sorry, I just forget you haven't been around much. Mr. Hagan's getting himself involved in a business down the road near the intersection. He's buyin' into NIPPER'S."

"Who's Nipper?"

'Well, he owns the liquor store over there. 'Course I don't drink, so I've never been inside. But it's where Mrs. Hagan used to buy her lottery tickets. I hear the owner's ill, so it's been hard keeping it going. Mr. Hagan is a friend, so he's buying in to help. Go on over and see it. It's on the way to the highway."

"A liquor store? He's calling it HAGAN'S HAVEN?"

"Said he didn't want to waste the sign," Moses said. "You know Mr. Hagan. Probably thinks it's a funny change from this place. At least it isn't on our road."

Moses went to find the Christmas lights while the workers installed the neon star. Toby was right, It faced the water and wouldn't be very visible from the hotel. Nodding admired the STILLWATERS sign. It was larger than the old one, but still modest.

Finally, Nodding couldn't stand it anymore. He found Moses in the garage and asked how to find the liquor store. He climbed into the Forester and drove back into Port Medway.

Instead of turning left at the intersection, he turned right, toward the lighthouse. Just around a bend he saw what looked like an old general store on his right. The sign company truck was parked in front, and the workers were taking down the old sign.

"Dave! You all settled in?" Hagan looked like a different man. His hair was cut, his beard was trimmed, and he was wearing a pair of khaki slacks instead of jeans. He looked ten pounds lighter.

"I didn't even recognize you," Nodding said, walking over to the ice machine where Hagan was standing.

"The wife went to work on me. Funny thing is, I don't mind it. I didn't even have to go on a diet or nothing to lose weight. Just started eating regular meals and avoiding truck stops. But it's still the real me. Pisses her off, though. All her idea, but she hasn't lost a pound herself. Says she feels like a stuffed Thanksgiving turkey."

"Moses says you're buying this place."

"Just a partner for now," Hagan said. "Come on in and meet Nipper."

He took a look at the sign being hoisted into place by a small crane on the truck, nodded at the workers, then opened the door and went inside. To Nodding's surprise, what had looked like a modest frame building had been extended back, making for a large retail space.

"Wow," Nodding said. "This place is big."

"Largest in the area," a female voice said.

Nodding turned and saw a smiling blonde woman at the cash register. She had her hair in a ponytail and wore a tight blue NIPPER'S golf shirt.

"Nipper was here before the province tightened up on sales. There's no NSLC outlet nearby, so we slowly got bigger, especially with craft beers. Can I help you find something?"

"Nah, he's with me," Hagan said. "Dave Nodding, meet Jody. Dave's running the conference centre."

"Oh yeah?" Jody said. "I've never been in there, but I hear it's nice. Me and you religious dudes don't have much in common, but you guys buy a lot of vodka every summer."

"Dave's okay. Guy named Belpre Tobias is the preacher,"

"Random," Jody put a piece of gum into her mouth and smiled. "When he gets too preachy, you just come over here and see us."

"Come on back and meet Nipper," Hagan said. "He started this place with just one room and expanded bit by bit. His cooler alone holds six hundred cases of beer."

"Does he really sell that much?" Nodding followed Hagan back through the store to a small office.

"Not this time of year, so he cuts his inventory. But come summer, he'll be packed all day. Folks between Bridgewater and Liverpool know to come here. But he won't handle cannabis. He sticks to alcohol."

"That would be a whole new set of problems, I guess."

"Before we go in, I gotta tell you." Hagan lowered his voice. "Nipper don't walk too good these days, so he won't stand up to shake hands or anything."

"Okay," Nodding said and followed Hagan into the office.

A large PRIVATE sign was on the door. Inside were a desk and two small easy chairs. Two television monitors were mounted to the wall behind the desk, and a stack of liquor posters and price lists was on the floor between the chairs. Nipper sat behind the desk in a wheelchair.

"Nipper, want you to meet a friend." Hagan turned to introduce Nodding.

"Davey," said the man behind the desk. He looked to be in his sixties, plump, with grey hair in a military cut, wearing wire-rimmed glasses. His face was pink, and as he smiled his eyes squinted closed and his lips pulled back until his gums were showing. "Chet's told me about you, and of course I heard Jody flirting with you out front."

He waved at the screens behind him, and Nodding noticed Jody biting her fingernail and then squinting at the camera.

"Nice to meet you," Nodding said, reaching across the desk to shake hands. Nipper smiled, then pulled a peanut butter cup out of his desk drawer and ripped it open.

"I worked for Nipper a few summers, back before my pa died," Hagan said. "Stopped in to say hello a couple of months ago and now I'm gonna be a damned partner."

"It's that or sell out to a stranger," Nipper said, patting the arms of his wheelchair. "This ain't a business you can run from one of these. Now I hire help for the summers, but it's getting harder. So when Chet came along I snagged him fast." He nodded at the chairs. "Grab a seat, boys."

Nodding settled into a chair and Hagan sprawled into the other.

"Liquor delivery due in about an hour, son," Nipper said. "Will the sign truck be out of the way?"

"Should be gone any minute," Hagan said. "Forklift is parked at the loading dock, and I got the order sheets ready to check off." He glanced at Nodding. "Time to build up stock for the summer people."

"I've been at this thirty years," Nipper said, smiling again as he finished his candy bar. "Great business. Everybody loves to drink."

He chuckled and glanced at Nodding. "Well, almost. I don't see all of your guests here, but some do stop in. And Beulah Hagan was a regular."

"I bet she wouldn't approve of our new sign," Hagan said.

"Won't people think you're gone, with your old sign gone?" Nodding said. "It's not a name you hear often."

"I guess maybe," Nipper said. "My father gave it to me. My real name is Floyd Eisenhower. Now, Daddy was from Newfoundland, and he thought I sounded like a mosquito when I cried. Nipper is what the Newfies call a big mosquito, so the name stuck."

He pulled a chocolate bar out of his drawer, put it on his desk, and began tapping it with his finger.

"Nipper had an older brother," Hagan said. "They were partners for several years when the store opened."

"Yep," Nipper said. "Lloyd was two years older than me. My parents thought I was gonna be a girl and had Flora picked out as my name. But I came along and they couldn't think straight, so they picked a name close to Lloyd's."

A buzzer sounded and Nodding looked at the television sets. A man was looking at shelves of bottles.

"Looking for wine," Hagan said. "I'll go see if I can help him." He stood up and left the office.

"Son, this is what I mean," Nipper said. "I need Chet to help the customers. That personal touch means a lot to folks."

"What about Jody?" Nodding said.

"I bought the latest cash register I could find, one with a scanner. Jody still messes it up. She doesn't know beans about what we have in stock and probably never will. But she's pretty and she flirts with the old men, and that's how she manages. If I was to let her go, I'd have a bunch of geezers protesting out front the next day."

He turned in his chair and looked at the television screens. "Besides, she's a sweet little thing to look at." He swung back around and tackled the candy bar on his desk.

Nodding saw Hagan on the screen, pointing out a section of the shelves to the man, who then picked out a bottle. They watched Jody ring up the sale and smile at the customer.

"I turn the sound down usually," Nipper said. "She sings to herself when she's bored, and the child is tone deaf. But mercy, those rap songs have some interesting words."

"That was simple," Hagan said, coming back into the office. "They've got the sign up and the wiring is almost finished." He smiled at Nodding. "Nipper damned near had me convinced to call the store the LONG BRANCH. Said he'd get a life size cut out of James Arness for the front. But I realized "Gunsmoke" has been off the air so long people wouldn't remember."

"I'd better get going," Nodding said. "Toby's coming in tonight, and I want his signs working when he gets here."

"You two get together and look through the storage barn by the house," Hagan said. "See if there's anything left of the parade float out there."

"Parade float?"

"Every year Liverpool has a parade for Canada Day. Lots of kids on bikes and bands and floats from hotels and businesses. Nipper had me get his out of storage, and we'll be fixing it up."

"Son, it's the social event of the summer," Nipper said. "Says a lot about the area right there. But it's a lot of fun and it's a good way to get to know us locals."

"I'll check it out," Nodding said. "Sounds interesting." He shook hands with Nipper. "Nice to meet you."

"You come back now, Davey. I won't be stopping by your place, so don't be a stranger here. An old guy like me needs company now and then."

He looked back at the screens where Jody was glancing down inside her shirt. "Mercy."

"You ain't old if you notice that," Hagan said.

"I feel old," Nipper said, nodding at the monitor. "Days like this."

"I'll see you to the door," Hagan said, leading the way up to the front of the store.

"Nice to meet you, Jody," Nodding said.

"Dude," she said, shaking her pony tail. "Come back and see me."

"Nipper has the sugars," Hagan said when they were outside. "Damn fool won't stop eating candy. He drinks soda, too, and just makes it worse. I keep talking to him about it, but in the middle of our conversation he'll pull out a candy bar. His brother Lloyd already died of a heart attack. He's all alone and eating himself to death. Shit, Dave, I don't know what to do, but he was real good to me when I was a teenager. I feel I owe him something, you know?"

"So you don't really want the liquor store?"

"Hell, no. I told him I didn't have the money, that it was tied up in the conference centre, and he said money wasn't an issue. Shit. I mean, damn, he's gonna come right out and give me the store soon. He needs help and he's lonely."

"You having any fun with it?" Nodding asked.

"Sure I am," Hagan said. "Guess that's another reason why I'm here. Keeps me busy, now I don't have to work. Wait 'til you see the float he's designing. It's gonna be a riot, come Canada Day."

"I'll stop back soon," Nodding said "Have fun working with Jody. How old is she, anyway?"

"Twenty-two, and damn sweet to look at, but there ain't nobody home, Dave," Hagan said, shaking his head. "Nipper don't care. She's got him wrapped around her little finger. You oughta see what she does on that camera when she thinks he's the only one watching."

"No thanks. I've got a job to concentrate on. My boss is one of those no fun, all business guys, you know.

"Oh yeah. Had a dispatcher like that for awhile at Melchior. Them guys is horrible." He winked and went back into the store.

Nodding watched the workmen testing the sign for a few minutes. They had HAGAN'S HAVEN flashing in red and yellow when he climbed into the Forester and drove home.

20: Funny thing, though

Nodding got back to the centre by four. Moses was gone, but had left a note with the mail, saying the sign and star were connected to an electronic sensor and would come on at dark. He would drive over to check it.

There were some notes from local furniture stores and one re-servation request, and then Nodding noticed the postcard.

It had a picture of Cuba, but the postmark was from Halifax. All it said was: "Keeping a low profile. It's working. Mum's the word."

There was no signature, but he knew Mrs. Saks was back at work. "She ought to get some monitors like Nipper," he said.

He put the postcard in his top desk drawer and went upstairs to make some dinner. He'd have it ready when Toby arrived.

The next morning Nodding and Toby were scheduled to inter-view two applicants for the open desk clerk position. They had breakfast and coffee in the kitchen, but still had an hour before their first interview, so Nodding told Toby about the Canada Day parade.

"What a way to spread God's word." Toby rubbed his hands to-gether, looking out at the ocean. "Little kids throwing out candy and praising."

"There's supposed to be at least part of a float out in the storage garage."

"Let's run out and take a look," Toby said. "We have a little time."

"I don't know if it's locked," Nodding said, grabbing his keys.

"One of these should fit, if it is."

They hurried down the steps, grabbing their jackets from the lobby, then went out into the April chill. It was a clear day and promised to be warmer by afternoon.

"I haven't even looked inside the place," Toby said. "I thought it was all lawn mowers and other equipment."

They walked past the house and back to the garage, which was a small white barn. There was a lock on the hasp but it wasn't snapped shut, so Nodding pulled it out and slid the door open.

"Well, I was right. We have some lawn mowers." Toby stared at the collection of mowers just inside the door. "Seven. We have seven lawn mowers."

"And a truck, and all kinds of boxes," Nodding said.

"There," Toby said, pointing to the back of the room. A large wooden platform was leaning against the far wall. "It either fits over the truck or the truck tows it."

They walked back to get a closer look.

"It needs a few repairs," Nodding said. "Looks like it's missing some boards. Let's ask Moses about it. It might be fun to see what we could do."

"We could make an ark," Toby said, then shook his head. "Nah. Too gloomy. We have to spread the Good Word."

"Let's get back and look official for the interviews."

"You ask the questions," Toby said. "I've always been on the other side of the table. Besides, they'll be working for you."

"They'll be working with all of us," Nodding said, sliding the garage door shut. "We should hire someone you feel comfortable with, too."

"I'm all excited by the float idea," Toby said. "I feel like a kid before the talent show."

"Did you sing?"

"I played the trumpet. Mighty poor at it, too."

They got to the main building and had just taken off their jackets when the first applicant arrived.

Ronnie Leister was a blond, slender young man of twenty. He'd been working at a motel in Bridgewater until mid-winter and since then had been busing tables in Liverpool. He was articulate, cheerful, and experienced.

"So why'd you leave the job in Bridgewater?" Nodding looked down at the resume.

"I didn't leave. I was fired," he said. "When you call for a reference, they'll say I was a good worker but I missed too many days. Last winter was simply awful with snow and ice, and at times I couldn't even get to the highway, let alone the Bridgewater streets."

"I appreciate your honesty," Nodding said.

"Where do you live, son?" Toby said. "Will getting here be a problem?"

"It's no problem in good weather," he said, crossing his legs and smoothing his pant leg. "And if the job lasts into winter, I'll hopefully have a more reliable vehicle by then." He smiled. "I live in Mahone Bay, in a dreadful little apartment."

Nodding promised to call Ronnie early in the week, after he checked his references. They all shook hands, and Nodding saw the young man to the door.

"Seems like a bright kid," Toby said. "Almost too bad, because Jean had someone she wanted me to mention if he wasn't any good."

"You should have said something," Nodding said. "Someone you know is always better than a total stranger."

"No big deal. Jean didn't mention her until we had these interviews lined up. Just some friend I haven't even met." He looked at his watch. "This Sylvia lady's almost ten minutes late."

"Well, let's give her a little more time, but that could make our decision easier."

"Never was late for an appointment," Toby said. "I always try to be early."

"Ronnie was right on time. Even dressed up a bit, with a tie and jacket."

"Even then he was a bit dainty."

"Would that bother you?" Nodding said. "Would it make a difference if he came to work here?"

"No, it would not. A lot of Christians turn out to be prejudiced against people of different colours or beliefs or how they deal with their genders. I've studied on the Bible, and it never gives any reason for such views. I figure if anything is a sin, it's having hateful feelings. So I try not to judge, Dave. I treat everybody with the love Jesus sends my way. That's what it's all about."

"So you could work with him?"

"No problem."

"Good enough for me," Nodding said. "Funny thing, though. Moses said the roads weren't too bad this winter along the south shore."

He picked up the desk phone and dialed.

"Hi, Virginia. Dave Nodding. Toby and I just interviewed a young man from Mahone Bay. Do you or Toby know anyone up that way?" He winked at Toby. "His name is Ronnie Leister. Okay, thanks."

He hung up and smiled. "Virginia says between the two of them they know everybody in Mahone Bay."

"Wouldn't doubt it for a minute," Toby said. "Think the coffee's still warm?"

He took their mugs up to the kitchen. Just as he came back and settled into his chair, the telephone rang.

Nodding picked it up and took notes while he spoke with Virginia, Finally he said, "That does it. Thanks for checking." He hung up and looked at Toby.

"Knew it was too good to be true," Toby said. "Your expression says it all."

"He missed work because he was held by the RCMP up there for vandalism three times. He gets drunk almost every night, and his car is unreliable because he's hit mailboxes several times, deliberately."

"Guess his gender preferences won't be an issue," Toby said. "How about you let me call him with the bad news? Maybe I can slip in a word for the truth and Jesus while I'm at it."

"My pleasure," Nodding said, handing him the application. "And no sign of this Sylvia lady." He looked at his watch. "So, what about your wife's friend?"

"You may not want to even consider her. Her name's Mackenzie, and I guess she's almost thirty. Got married and pregnant early and has been working as a bank clerk. Husband left suddenly last fall, which leaves her stuck paying the mortgage and trying to support her son. So she's moving into a little apartment and selling the house. Jean likes her and figured she needed a change, even if just for the summer."

"You guys know her from church?"

"Partly. She comes every now and then. Her son comes to the church after-school daycare, so Jean got to know her that way."

"If you think she's reliable, let's see if she's interested." Nodding thought for a moment. "She'll be two hours or more from home. That would be a problem."

"I thought of that," Toby said. "Jean and I can work things out with housing. They could live with us."

"No," Nodding said. "That house is for your family. If she's coming to work here, we have two furnished apartments that are empty. We'll give her one if she's interested."

"Man, I appreciate this, Dave. Maybe Jean and her can come down this weekend with the kids."

"Sounds good. It's time to get things rolling around here. We have our first guests coming in nine days."

Nodding worked in the kitchen the next day, getting ready for food deliveries. At noon, Toby came in to say his family would be coming Saturday morning, along with Mackenzie and her son, Wyatt. They decided that since the apartments hadn't been cleaned, Mackenzie and her son should stay in one of the motel rooms, while Toby's family would try out their new house. Toby said Virginia had worked two days to get the house cleaned. He had asked if he could move his things in that afternoon.

"She still wanted to wax the floor in one room," he said. "I offered to help, but she told me to get out and do some 'man's work.' I swear, Dave, that woman knows how to give orders. She could whip any truck terminal into shape right quick."

Toby made himself a ham and cheese sandwich and took it with him to work in the chapel. Nodding was satisfied with the kitchen, so he took off to do some shopping.

He stopped at a farm market Virginia had shown him and bought some chicken. Then he drove to the supermarket in Liverpool for vegetables and breakfast supplies. He and Toby had been enjoying cereal and coffee, but there were kids arriving tomorrow, and he thought pancakes might be more interesting.

The kitchen had no cooking wine, so he stopped at Nipper's on his way home. Hagan's truck wasn't in the lot, but Jody was behind the counter, chewing gum and looking bored.

"Mr. Hagan went to the bank," she said. "But Nipper's out back in the beer cooler." She popped a quick pink bubble and winked at him. "Tired of the holy rollers yet?"

"They're getting pretty wild," he said. "Sent me over for some Marsala." She kept chewing but didn't say anything. "It's a kind of wine."

"It's over there somewhere," she said, pointing at the wine room. "Here I thought you'd come back just to see me."

"I did. The wine's just an excuse."

He smiled and wandered over to the wine section. There were signs indicating the imported area, and pretty soon he found what he wanted. He shook his head, thinking how easy it was to flirt with someone he had no interest in, yet how awkward he had felt with Jenny. It made no sense.

Nodding left the wine at the counter with Jody went to the beer cooler. He found Nipper, with a cane hanging on his arm, holding a clipboard and counting cases of cold beer. He had puffy brown slippers shaped like dog faces on his feet, with little red tongues sticking out where his toes were.

"Davy! Nice to see you, son." He saw Nodding's glance and waved the clipboard. "Don't you say a word. These are the only darn things I own that don't hurt my feet. Jody bought them for me last Christmas."

"Just stopped by to pick up some wine and say hello."

"I was thinking," Nipper said, pulling a chocolate bar from his shirt pocket. "If you folks are interested, I could get some non-alcoholic wine in stock. Your people might enjoy some as a treat." He unwrapped the candy and took a bite.

"I'll talk with Toby. He'll have a better idea than I would about it."

"Good enough," Nipper said, licking his fingers. "Mercy. I'm being rude." He pulled out a peanut butter cup from his shirt pocket and offered it. "Little burst of energy?"

"No thanks. I better get going. Tell Hagan I said hi."

"Be happy to. He should be back directly. Mercy, that boy spends more time in here than I do some days."

"I guess he's interested in learning the business," Nodding said.

"I hope so," Nipper said, looking down at his clipboard. "Could just be his wife, though. That Lucille's a real number."

"I haven't met her."

"I only did once," Nipper said. "Generally a happy woman, but she has the notion he needs to improve himself. When he stays home she starts in about joining health clubs and eating celery and such, so the poor boy just has to escape. She stopped by once and frowned the whole time she sat in the office. I half expected a thunderstorm right indoors. I don't think she'll be back anytime soon. We're just not classy enough."

He shook his head and smiled. "You like westerns as much as Chet, Davy?"

"Grew up on them. Old reruns mostly."

"I was watching the cable last night," Nipper said. "That 'Bonanza' was one hell of a show, you know? Had a little bit of everything. Mercy."

"I always wanted to go visit the Ponderosa. My parents told me it was probably torn down when they stopped filming, back when they were kids. But I saw that map and believed it was real."

"Never did get tired of that Hoss. Mercy. He kept his sense of humour through most everything."

"Great show," Nodding said.

He saw Nipper glance down at his clipboard and start counting, so he retreated to the cash register.

"You spend much time in Bridgewater?" Jody said, putting his wine in a bag.

"No. Just passed through a few times. I spend more time in Liverpool."

"There's a new place opening this summer. Gonna be radical. Called Floaters. It's on the river, and you can sit out on an inner tube and they'll bring you drinks. And the tubes are tied down, so you won't float away."

"I'll have to check it out."

"They won't open until July, dude," she said. "The water's too cold now."

She handed him the bag "Maybe I'll see you there when the weather gets hot."

"I'll look for you," Nodding said. "Don't work too hard."

21: Jesus doesn't mind

That night Nodding hooked up his television to the cable outlet in his apartment. Mrs. Hagan had protected her guests from the tube, but she thought differently about her employees. The apartments and house all had cable hookups, and Nodding was grateful.

He was happy to be back in touch with the world, but after a few minutes he switched it off. He learned the headlines each day through his computer and radio and felt fine without the gory details. Life at the shore was having an effect on him, he realized.

The next morning Nodding mopped out the walk-in freezer and cold box. The big deliveries would start Monday, and he had to be ready. He checked the mail, sorted the reservation requests, and entered them into the computer. He printed out postcard replies and was about to break for lunch when Toby came into the office with his wife.

"Dave, this here is Jean, the one and only, God love her." Toby had his arm around her, and his face was flushed with pride.

Jean Tobias was a skinny blonde in her early forties who smiled with her mouth shut when she shook Nodding's hand. She was dressed in jeans, a sweater, and sneakers.

"You picked a great weekend," Nodding said. "Supposed to hit fifteen or even more today, so you and the kids can hike out on the beach."

"I can hardly wait," Jean said. Nodding saw her teeth were crooked. "The kids were wild the whole way down. They just can't wait for summer away from the city."

"I had the girls go check out the house," Toby said. "I figured we could have a little family prayer meeting when Jean and I get there, so the kids should have a little time to explore first."

"Toby showed Mackenzie and Wyatt their room," Jean said. "This whole hotel is just beautiful."

After they left, Nodding drove to the town intersection, where there was a mailbox. He dropped the reservation responses in, then drove back to start dinner.

From the dining room he caught sight of Toby and his family on the beach. The girls, Christine and Mary, were both blondes and cute. He smiled, watching Toby hold hands with Jean as they strolled.

Nodding saw a woman jogging down the beach with a young boy and went over to the windows to see her more clearly. She waved at Toby and Jean, so he assumed she was Mackenzie. She was taller than Jean, slender, with brown hair. The salt air had clouded the windows slightly, so he couldn't make out her features. Her little boy, Wyatt, was the same size as five-year-old Mary and also had brown hair.

Nodding watched them for a few minutes, then went back to his work in the kitchen.

At six, everyone met in the dining room for the first "official" dinner at STILLWATERS. Nodding set a special table for the kids and served them chicken strips and french fries. He knew it was unimaginative, but they loved it.

Mackenzie Pearse was attractive, athletic, and unpretentious. She shook hands with Nodding with a firm grip and joked with Toby about the need for dinner reservations. She got along well with Jean, too, and Nodding relaxed a bit about her moving in for the summer. She was intelligent enough to know what she was do-ing.

"Could we have grace, please?" Toby stood up and bowed his head. Even the children got quiet.

"Jesus, we're together now to make this a blessed summer for all sorts of pilgrims. We ask you to bless this chicken and us too, so we can serve you better. We thank you for our blessings and for Beu-lah Hagan's good fortune."

"I thought she died," one of the children whispered.

"We ask this in your name, Amen." Toby glared at the children and sat down.

"How can you get good fortune when you're dead?" Christine said.

"Sweetie, she went to heaven to be with Jesus," Jean said.

"Hope everything is good," Nodding said, handing serving dishes to Jean to pass around the table.

He had tried some possible summer recipes, stuffing baked potatoes with cheddar and lightly seasoning some green beans with a hint of ginger. After grilling the chicken he had simmered it in a mushroom sauce featuring the Marsala. They were recipes he had never prepared for students in Antigonish.

"Man, this chicken is special," Toby said. "I'll be a blimp if the food's this good all summer."

"Now I don't know, Toby," Jean said. "Doesn't say much for my cooking."

"I love your cooking, sweetheart," Toby said, still chewing. "We just eat a little less fancy."

"I wish I could cook this way," Mackenzie said, trying the beans. "But once you get beyond salt and pepper, I'm lost."

"Just experiment," Nodding said. "It's fun to try new things, but they don't always work out."

"You're just being nice," Jean said. "Have you ever bombed with a recipe?"

"Sure. I made a vegetable stew once with strips of grilled tofu. I threw it into the compost after tasting it."

"I can only imagine," Toby said. "Like linoleum sticks. What kind of mind would come up with something like that?"

"Vegetables are good for you," Christine said from her table. "We're learning about them in school."

"You're right, honey," Toby said. "Maybe that stew just had a bad mix of vegetables." He took another chicken thigh and smiled at it. "But this chicken is a winner."

When the kids finished their dinner, Nodding gave them ice cream for dessert. Then they rambled out to the gazebo to look at the blue star while the adults had coffee and fresh rhubarb pie.

"Lordy," Toby said finally. "I don't think I can move."

"Lucky you're not sleeping in here," Jean said. "No midnight snacks tonight."

"Mackenzie, you can just wander down here any night this summer for leftovers," Toby said. "I don't think I could resist that temptation."

"I run every day just to keep my weight down," she said, smiling. "So I'll have to stay away from the temptation. I'll be fine as long as I don't find a bag of chips lying around."

"Have you always been a jogger?" Jean said. "I could never get myself to stick with it."

"I started in high school. I ran cross country. Then I stopped, but after Wyatt was born I started again. When Rick and I were having troubles, it got me away from the house for a while each day."

"Land around here is ideal for running," Toby said. "Some hills, but not much traffic."

"Talk about traffic, you folks open up next weekend," Jean said.

"We do," Nodding said. "I think we're ready. Virginia and her daughters are coming in to make beds and dust this week, and the kitchen staff starts Thursday. I haven't been through it before, but I think we're prepared."

"Are you full?" Mackenzie asked.

"We still have some rooms. We didn't send out any reminders this winter, so things are a little slow. But that's fine for the first few weekends. By late May we're booked all week long with over half the rooms full."

"We have a good preacher comin' in next weekend," Toby said. "Reverend Angus Summers from Cape Breton. Talked to him on the phone, and he's been our Easter preacher for six years now. He'll hold a sunrise service right in here, so's we can see the beach and all and not freeze. His church up near Louisbourg is still surrounded by snow, so the Easter turnout is tiny. That's why he can travel down here."

"I want to thank you all for offering me a place here," Mackenzie said. "I really think it's what Wyatt and I need." She looked at Nodding and their eyes met. She smiled.

"I found you daycare until July at the Anglican church up the road," Toby said. "After that, we'll have our own up and running here, with Jean."

"We appreciate you coming with so little notice," Nodding said. "But by next weekend your apartment will be ready."

"Dave says he's rented out the third apartment," Toby said. "Don't look like we'll need it for any of us."

"Lady from New Brunswick called and talked with Virginia," Nodding said. "She wanted a place with a view of the beach and an elevator because she doesn't get around very well and might need room service. Took it from mid-June to mid-July and she's paying in advance."

"Here's to our summer and STILLWATERS," Toby said, raising his coffee cup. "I can feel it all over. My spirit is glowin'. Jesus is with us tonight."

"Amen," Jean said. She looked over at Nodding and smiled. "He gets a little carried away sometimes, as you probably know. Then you just have to talk reasonable, like when he wanted us to pray in the parking lot today."

"I didn't mind," Mackenzie said.

"The kids did," Jean said. "They'd been in the car more than two hours already. And I didn't want to dirty my pants on that damp gravel, either."

"Jesus doesn't mind a little discomfort or mess," Toby said.

"Jesus doesn't do the wash," Jean said. "The floor in the house worked just fine for the prayer, right?" She reached over and squeezed his hand, and he smiled.

"Yes, dear," Toby said. "Kinda puts things back in perspective."

He looked up as the kids came bursting through the door, and the meal came to a natural end.

Sunday was quiet. Nodding stayed behind when everyone went to church and then out to lunch in Liverpool. He took the time to go for a walk on the beach. It would be his last chance for peace and quiet for a while, and he enjoyed himself. The weather was warming up, and the other wanderers he met on the beach had friendly smiles.

Jean, Mackenzie, and the children left later in the afternoon for home, and Toby spent the evening by himself, settling into the house.

Nodding explored the barn, but found nothing exciting beyond lawn mowers and the float platform, and finally retreated to his apartment.

When he got to his door he found a crayon picture of waves taped to it. One of the children had written, "Thank you David. Jesus Loves YOU."

He left it on his door,

Nodding enjoyed the week before Easter because he was too busy to worry about the opening. He and Toby coordinated the meal and activity schedules. He met with the three cooks and the meal servers, who came by for an orientation meeting Tuesday. University and high school students would round out the staff in July, once things got busy.

Food deliveries began Monday, and by Wednesday all but the dairy products were in.

Virginia ordered him out of the kitchen Wednesday afternoon, saying it needed one last cleaning. "It's always this busy at first," she said. "And every year it works out. Just you wait." She put her hands on her hips and inspected the grill.

"I emptied the grease trap yesterday," Nodding said.

"I'm not blind. Last year it was a mess. I had to come in early a few times to get it done before they cooked breakfast. All that fat sitting in there got me to worrying about fires and mice and all sorts of bugs." She raised her hands and waved him away.

"I'll be in the office," he said.

"Oh, I forgot," she said. "Who's in charge of public relations?"

"Here?" he said. "We don't have anyone, but I guess I'd be the one."

"Lady called this morning from the *Chronicle Herald*. She said she was returning a call from public relations. I told her I had no idea what it was about, so I took her number and put it on your desk."

The Halifax number was for a reporter named Amanda. He called her and explained who he was.

"Thanks for calling me back," she said. "I was really trying to get back to the woman who called me and left a message. Her name came up as 'private,' and the message cut off just as she was leaving her number."

"That's a little strange," Nodding said. "We don't have anyone here doing public relations right now."

"Her name is, uh, Ms. Elliot. She wanted me to drive down and interview two truck drivers you have working there."

"Well, we do have two former drivers here. Mr. Hagan is the centre owner, and Mr. Tobias is our program director."

"If I'm down your way next week, might I stop by and chat with them?"

"I'm certain Mr. Tobias would be happy to meet you," he said. "Mr. Hagan isn't involved with our operation, so he's rarely here." He couldn't think of anyone who might think she was doing public relations.

"I have a meeting in Bridgewater on Wednesday," she said. "Could I call Tuesday to schedule a visit?"

"Fine," Nodding said. "Did this Mrs. Elliot say anything else? We really have no one by that name here."

"Maybe she's with an agency?" she said. "She did say she was calling from the road."

Nodding thanked her and hung up, and then the name came back. Mrs. Saks had set this up on purpose. What was she up to? He found her number on his phone and called it, but there was no answer.

"Wait a minute," he said to himself. He typed SAKS and ELLIOT into the reservations computer, but both were unknown.

"Just call me." he told the blank computer screen. "Tell me what you're up to."

Nothing happened, so he typed in the weekend date and reviewed the pending arrivals.

22: Don't like change much

On Thursday Toby drove up to the Walmart in Bridgewater to buy some white shirts. Then he stopped at the fabric centre and bought black fabric to drape around the chapel for Friday. Nodding found him there that afternoon on a ladder, replacing a light bulb.

"The spotlight on the pulpit just up and died," Toby said. "Tomorrow evening will be dark enough in here with the mourning cloth and all. We need the spotlight, and I figured Moses was too busy."

"You've done a great job," Nodding said, looking around. "This place is spotless."

Toby had scrubbed the wooden floors himself, then refinished them when he wasn't happy with their look. He had carefully cleaned the stained glass window showing the crucifixion and polished the brass candlesticks. The pews had been waxed, and even the folding chairs had been scrubbed.

"I'm nervous," Toby said. "I've spent a full hour every morning talkin' with Jesus about this weekend, but I still keep thinking I'll forget something."

"The guests won't notice," Nodding said. "They'll be too impressed with all of the improvements."

"Everything in good shape with the rooms?" Toby climbed down and looked at his hands, checking for dust.

"Virginia says we're fine, Moses wanted to paint three ceilings, and they should be dry by tonight." He took a sheet of paper out of his pocket and unfolded it. "I got your note about refreshments for the Sunday reception."

"I couldn't find you, and Virginia wouldn't let me in the kitchen."

"She threw me out, too." Nodding said. "Anyway, we're all set. I ordered some things last week that we can use, like small pastries. We'll have fresh-baked cookies as well. But your note mentioned sardines."

"I guess we don't need 'em," Toby said. "I just thought something fancy like sardines all laid out on saltines would be a nice gourmet touch, being Easter and all."

"I think the pastries will be fancy enough. Sardines might not go smoothly with cookies and pastries."

"Never thought of that," Toby said. "It'd be like anchovies or hot peppers. I should have known you'd have it figured out better."

"Not always. How about I get some sardines and add them to the relish trays? We'll have saltines on the tables already for soup."

"Can you do it this fast? I don't want to cause problems or nothing. Will it mess up your budget?"

"We can afford some sardines. As long as they are in the relish dish, I can take care of it."

"Thanks, Dave," Toby said. "I just always thought sardines were kind of special."

"And we'll have them," Nodding said. "I'll get them this afternoon."

He left Toby polishing the candlesticks and drove to Liverpool. His experience with serving university students had taught him to be flexible, and he only hoped sardines would be his worst worry.

Mabel Holbert and her husband, Roy, were the first guests to check in Friday morning. Nodding was at the front desk when they arrived.

"We the first?" Mabel said. She had a carnation pinned to her red cloth coat. She pulled off her white scarf and handed it to Roy, who stood behind her. "Been first for six years now, and we want to keep up the tradition."

"You're first," Nodding said. He slid a registration form across the desk

"Why'd you go and change the name?" She reached into her purse for a pair of bifocals, stared at the form, then began to print her name.

"Mrs. Hagan passed away. We've changed a few things, but I believe you'll find them improvements."

"I doubt it," she said. "We come all the way from Pugwash every year, this weekend and one in August. Don't like change much, do we, Roy?"

"Looks the same to me." Roy was looking up at the painting behind the desk. He shrugged.

"Who's the preacher this weekend?" Mabel said, handing back the form. "Anyone good?"

"Reverend Summers is back," Nodding said.

"Now, he's too cheerful for my taste," Mabel said. "Always telling you to look up and have faith. What good is that when half the world will fry in hell? Right, Roy?"

"I like him," Roy said.

"You men," she said. "You serving chicken for Easter dinner?"

"Easter ham," Nodding said. "Same as always."

'That preacher makes you feel good after his sermons," Roy said.

"That's one good thing," Mabel said. "I hate chicken, unless it's fried crispy."

"Let's go see the room," Roy said, taking her arm.

"Better be clean," Mabel said. "I have an eye for dirt."

"She does," said Roy, leading her away from the desk. "Always has."

"Let us know if you find any problems," Nodding said.

Moses was coming in the front door and held it open for the

Holberts. He smiled at Nodding as they went out.

"Two years ago those folks had a flat tire and weren't the first," he said. "They stayed mad all weekend."

"Are all the guests like that?" Nodding said. He leaned over the desk to speak quietly.

"Some. Most are worse." He winked at Nodding. "That flower is plastic."

"Her carnation?"

"Fell off in the dining room last summer. Virginia made me take it to her room."

"This could be a long summer."

"Don't worry," Moses said. Just about everybody else who stays here is nice. Virginia calls that woman 'Witch Mabel.' Every time she talks to me I just smile and think of Mr. Holbert. He's the one has to go home with her after the weekend, poor fella."

He shook his head. "I caused some of the mess, though. I told her husband they were thinking of giving the guests who checked in first a free weekend. Since then they've been even worse."

Mackenzie, who had told everyone to just call her 'Kenzie', arrived later in the afternoon to take over the desk, while Nodding went to work on dinner. The local cooks were experienced, calm, and friendly. He felt himself relax as the afternoon passed without problems.

Saturday was cloudy and warmer, but the rain held off. Guests wandered on the beach or sat in the gazebo and watched the water. Dinner went smoothly, and Reverend Masters held a prayer meeting and hymn-sing afterwards in the chapel.

Nodding helped Toby move an altar and flowers into the dining room for the sunrise service, and they sat down for a cup of coffee afterwards.

"It's working out," Nodding said. "I'm glad we're not full this weekend, but we'll be ready by summer."

"I love it," Toby said. "I don't think I've ever been this busy, but God's work don't wear you out."

He gulped the rest of his coffee and stood up. "Angus promised to sit down after the singing and give me some ideas for the summer," he said. "I'd better get back."

"See you in the morning," Nodding said.

He closed up the kitchen, then strolled out to the gazebo to get a breath of fresh air. Under the blue star's pale light he turned, looked back at the hotel, and smiled.

It was the right move, coming here.

Toby was right too. The work was hard, but he was happy doing it, and he found himself looking forward to each day. He took a deep breath of the salt air and turned back to look at the water. The waves were gentle tonight, mostly hissing, their foam glowing blue from the star.

Nodding stretched and went in and up the steps. When he got upstairs Kenzie was polishing the door to her apartment.

"Didn't Virginia's crew clean it?" he said.

"It was spotless," she said. "But I thought this pretty old wood could look so much nicer with a little lemon oil." She stepped back and Nodding smiled. The grain stood out and the wood glistened.

"Can I offer you a cup of tea?" she said. "The water's already hot."

"Some other night I'd love it," he said. "But this has been a very long day."

She smiled as he opened his own door, which looked faded and dry by contrast. "I'll do yours tomorrow," she said. "Wyatt wants to get up for the sunrise service, so I better get some rest myself."

23: Eggs

Sunday was clear and cool. The sunrise service went smoothly, and Nodding had a buffet breakfast ready when Reverend Masters finished. Another service with a sermon was scheduled for the chapel at ten. That gave Nodding and his crew time to clean up and prepare Easter dinner.

"Jesus is risen!" Toby shouted, coming into the kitchen just before dinner was ready. "Happy Easter, everyone."

"It's a beautiful day," Nodding said, waving a handful of parsley in greeting.

Toby ducked out to welcome guests and lead the blessing, and the major meal of the weekend was underway.

When the guests started moving toward the dessert table, Nodding went down to relieve Kenzie at the desk. After she ate, they'd both be on hand for the rush at checkout. He took a mug of coffee down, thinking it would be quiet for a bit.

Just as Kenzie went up the stairs, Hagan came in the front door, carrying a basket of candy. "Just came to wish you all a Happy Easter and to drop off a little something from Nipper."

He was dressed in a sport shirt and slacks and looked even slimmer than he had two weeks ago.

"Thanks," Nodding said, taking the basket and putting it on the counter. "The weekend's been great."

"Figured it would be." Hagan pointed at the basket. "Nipper says the eggs wrapped in red were the best. He musta ate five of them while we were making up the basket."

"I'll stop by to thank him this week. He's gone out of his way to be friendly."

"He's a good man," Hagan said.

"Hurry, Roy, I think we're first." Mabel Holbert was coming down the steps, still clutching her napkin. She was wearing a bright green dress with a tiny yellow hat pinned to her hair. Her purse was also green, but clashed with her dress, and the fake carnation was on her chest.

Roy came into sight a moment later, grasping a coffee cup and trying to sip from it as he followed his wife down the steps. His grey suit was too big in the waist, making him look creased where his belt pulled the cloth together.

"Lookee here," Hagan said, nodding at the steps.

"Jesus has come," Mrs. Holbert said, reaching the bottom of the steps and waving her napkin. "Happy Easter!"

"Now, I been called a lot of names before," Hagan said, smiling.

"I hope we're first," she said, hurrying to the desk. "Do we get some of this candy? I could eat a whole package of those eggs my-self."

Hagan turned and looked away.

"Have one," Nodding said, pushing the basket forward.

"Come to check out," she said, taking three of the eggs. She handed one back to Roy, then turned again and gave him her nap-kin. "I miss the jelly beans," she said. "Last year every room had jelly beans."

"We had bowls of them on every table."

"Not in the rooms. You just had two little mints in each room. What's Easter without jelly beans?"

Nodding handed her the bill while she rummaged through her purse for her credit card. "I can't believe what things cost. Why, I remember when you could spend an entire week here for this."

She waved the bill at Nodding, then glanced over at Hagan. "Our bags are in the room," she told him. "Roy will show you where to put them." She began peeling the foil off of a candy egg. "Is it true we get a weekend free if we're first?"

"First you think I'm Jesus and then you want me to carry your suitcases?" Hagan said.

"I think this man's a guest," Roy said. "I'm sorry."

"Roy has a condition," Mabel said. "He shouldn't lift."

"I'll help you out, Roy," Hagan said, winking at Nodding. "It's Easter, and I'm not busy right now."

"You stay close to him, Roy," she said. "Mark nothing gets stolen, now."

"Now wait," Hagan said. "This is Easter, lady. I'm being friendly, but you keep saying ignorant things. I'm really trying to be good, but you're pushing it mighty hard."

"I don't trust anyone who doesn't follow Jesus," she said. "It's not you alone. You're just an atheist and you don't know better."

She opened her purse again and pulled out her glasses to check the bill. "That coloured man said you might let the first people have a free weekend."

"Don't worry about the bill," Hagan said. "We hired a group of nuns to be sure they were correct. And Moses is an African. That other term is hateful."

"God will strike you dead for such talk," she said, taking a step back. "Even if Catholics are misguided, they're still believers. "

"Come on, Roy, let's get the bags," Hagan said, shaking his head.

"They're just on the first floor," Roy said. "I'm sorry."

"Don't you go near our bags," Mabel said. "I don't trust you any-where close to my personal property with talk like that."

"May I be of service, Mrs. Holbert?" Moses had come in quietly and now stepped forward.

"I want this man removed at once," she said pointing at Hagan. "I plan to write the owner and complain about the rude bellboy as soon as we get home to Pugwash. As for you, we got excited last year when you told us about being first, and now everyone just stares at me when I mention it."

"I don't work here," Hagan said. "Save your ink. I'll leave."

"Beulah Hagan was a close friend of mine," Mabel said. "If she were here, you'd never be allowed in that front door."

"If she were here, I'd be over in Pugwash, too," Hagan said. "Makes sense you're a friend of hers. You're as full of it as she was."

He stepped up to the counter, took a foil covered candy egg from the basket, and put it on the counter in front of her.

"What's that for?" she said. She took her card out of the machine.

"I'm leaving," he said. "Moses will help Roy with your bags. Then you can get in the car, take this egg, and sit on it." He shook his head as he went out the door.

"That man," Mabel said, waving her finger at Nodding.

"You mean Mr. Hagan?" Moses said, smiling at Nodding. "Our new owner?"

"We only have three bags," Roy said. "I'm really sorry."

"We may have to stay home in August," Mabel said. "He'll run this place into the ground."

"He might be working here by then," Nodding said. "You'd have a chance to spend more time with him."

He saw Moses clamp his mouth shut and head for the suitcases with Roy.

Mrs. Holbert picked up her receipt, snatched the candy egg, and marched out of the lobby without another word.

After the next couple had checked out and left, Nodding looked around the lobby and took a deep breath.

The door opened and Hagan came back inside. "I'm sorry, Dave," he said. "I tried to shut up, but that old bitch just wouldn't quit. At least I didn't tell her she was full of shit. I had that much control."

"Don't worry," Nodding said. "I enjoyed every second of it."

"I'm serious, though. I didn't mean to say nothing bad. I won't stop by and mess things up unless you call me. I promise."

He looked at the basket, grabbed a few jelly beans, and took off.

The rest of the afternoon went smoothly, with the guests checking out after a fine weekend. By sunset everyone was gone except Toby and Nodding. Even Virginia and Moses had called it quits.

"We survived," Nodding said. He and Toby were behind the desk, nibbling at Hagan's basket.

"It's a sign," Toby said. "We're off to a good start and the summer ain't even here yet."

He stepped back from the basket and slapped his belly. "I gotta get away from this stuff. I been picking at candy all afternoon." He smiled and pointed at a red egg. "You think that woman's still settin' on her egg?"

"She probably made Roy do it," Nodding said.

"Jean and the kids are fixing to drive back. I'll go over and say goodbye."

"You did a great job this weekend," Nodding said. "Feel a little less nervous now?"

"Guess so. But it was only for two days in a row. Let's see how things get to be in June and July. I'll be put to the test more in summer."

Nodding closed up the office and climbed the stairs. He smiled to see his apartment door was oiled and polished,

For the next few weeks guests would be in for weekend visits. By next month they'd be open all week, and the summer would be in full swing. But it didn't scare him. The people working here were good at their jobs and he liked them. The summer reinforcements would help carry the heavy crowds.

This was going to work out after all.

~

Amanda called on Tuesday to arrange an interview with Toby. She had already reached Hagan at the liquor store, and he had agreed to stop by the next day to chat and have his picture taken. So on Wednesday Nodding made lunch for them while they waited for Amanda.

"I gotta get over to see your store," Toby said. "Jean told me to buy some lottery tickets when the jackpot gets high."

"Nipper's all excited," Hagan said, waving a french fry. "He's featuring a different Nova Scotia beer each week, one of those little gourmet kinds."

"Micro breweries are popular these days," Nodding said.

"We're putting in a new cooler up front just for them and European imports," Hagan said. "I told him people could find them back in our old cooler, but Nipper wants to be the best."

"I want to meet him," Toby said. "Sounds very interesting."

"I don't know," Hagan said. "He's cheerful, but he ain't a happy man. He's eating candy and chips and every night he orders pizza or fried stuff. Just watching him made me eat more healthy." He looked at his one remaining french fry. "Most of the time, anyway."

"Have you talked with him about it?" Toby said.

"You and me both know it won't do no good," Hagan said. "A growed man has to make his own choices. Nipper's been to the doctor. He's heard the talk."

"This weekend I had a long chat with Angus Masters," Toby said. "Made me feel a lot better about what I could do here and all. Put me at ease. Well, anyway, he told me a story about that fella from India, that Gandhi."

"I've heard of him," Hagan said. "That's about it."

"He was a great leader," Toby said. "Folks looked up to him. And one day this here woman brings a little kid in and asks Gandhi to tell her kid not to eat sugar."

"I don't think Nipper would go see him," Hagan said.

"This was awhile back," Toby said. "He's passed on now." He leaned forward, "Point is, this Gandhi sends her away for a few days. When she comes back with her kid, Gandhi looks at the boy and says 'Don't eat sugar no more.' So the mother looks at him and asks why she had to go away before. Gandhi looks at her and says, 'Two days ago I was still eating sugar.'"

"Good yarn, Preacher," Hagan said. " I ain't tryin' to clean up my life. It's just kinda working out. But I don't feel like I'm in a position to tell Nipper how to live anymore. I've tried, Think you could give it a shot?"

"I'll come meet him. Let's see where that takes us." He glanced at his watch. "I'll go down to the lobby. That reporter should be here soon."

Amanda showed up on time, armed with a tape recorder and a camera. She was a bubbly redhead in her mid twenties and she handled the interview well.

Nodding was impressed that she zeroed in on the truck drivers and their new careers at once, then let them digress a bit. She had heard about the parking lot gunfire in Antigonish and said she'd check the paper's records for the January coverage.

She took a picture of the two men together, then had Nodding join them for a photo outside in the gazebo. She said she'd let them know when the feature would run and chatted with Toby for a few minutes about the mysterious Ms. Elliot.

Then she left to go back to Halifax and her office.

"News must be scarce down here for us to make the paper," Toby said. "Wonder who this Elliot woman is, anyway?"

"I think I know," Nodding said. He explained about Elliot and Mrs. Saks and predicted they'd hear more from her in the future.

"Good woman," Hagan said, grabbing his windbreaker. "If she comes by, be sure to send her over to the store."

"As long as she comes without that pistol, I'd like to see her too," Toby said.

24: Don't blow my cover

By the next weekend Nodding felt at home in the kitchen. Kenzie had finished moving in and was settled, giving him more time away from the front desk. As the number of guests grew steadily, he fell into a routine he enjoyed. Each Monday he joined Toby, Moses, and Kenzie for lunch. They discussed the past week and planned ways to improve the operation.

Virginia declined to attend. "Cleaning doesn't need talk," she said. "If you find some dirt, just say so." But they rarely found anything that wasn't spotless.

By June first things were in full swing, and Nodding was impressed. He was ahead of his budget, the rooms were filling up fast, and Toby's program was keeping everyone busy and excited. Each weekend a different minister arrived to preach, in exchange for a mini-vacation, some bringing a busload of paying guests with them.

And then Amanda called and said the story was going to appear.

Sunday arrived, and Nodding found the *Chronicle-Herald* article online. The story made the first page of the Features section with two nice pictures. One was of Toby and Hagan, and the other was of the gazebo and beach. Nodding knew the article couldn't do anything but help business, because it played up the centre's reputation and program while highlighting Toby and Hagan.

Sure enough, the next day he fielded six reservation requests within an hour after breakfast.

On Wednesday Kenzie brought him a plain postcard, post-marked Halifax. All it said was: "THE NEWSPAPER GOT THINGS MOVING. THE CHASE IS ON. KEEP YOUR POWDER DRY."

"What's it mean?" Kenzie said, once he explained who it was from.

"God only knows," Nodding said. "She's convinced there's still a threat from our old neighbour, but I'm not sure about the whole newspaper connection. Wissam was never after me for anything."

"I think it's exciting. Who knows what might come in the mail tomorrow? This job is just great." She bestowed a wide smile on him before going back to the desk.

But nothing unusual came the next day, and Nodding filed the postcard with his earlier one. The conference centre was getting busier by the day, and there wasn't much free time for speculation. June had brought warmer weather, and summer was fast approaching.

Nodding spent a few weekday evenings wandering along the beach. He enjoyed the later sunsets and cool evening breezes and being able to stroll without meeting any other wanderers. On weekends, centre guests were frequent strollers.

He came into the lobby one evening after his walk and Kenzie waved him over to the desk. "She's here," she said. "And she's weird."

"The Greek lady?" For three days they had gotten calls from the woman who was renting the third apartment for a month. She had requested a bellboy be on duty when she arrived to carry her bags. She asked if there were any car rental agencies nearby. She asked about daily temperatures, so she could pack appropriately.

"She flew in a private plane into Yarmouth," Kenzie said. "Then she hired a cab to bring her up here, instead of renting a car." Kenzie looked around the lobby and lowered her voice. "I bet she's a movie actress or political figure."

"She look familiar?"

"No, but she was wearing a red wig and mirror sunglasses," Kenzie said. "The wig was pretty obvious. She's trying to disguise herself or she's some kind of nut."

"I'll have to be sure I see her tomorrow," he said. "But she can be as weird as she wants. She paid her bill in advance." He went into his office, wondering if she was a famous widow.

Later that evening Nodding closed up the office and headed upstairs. He passed by the guest apartment, but it was quiet and a 'Do Not Disturb' sign hung from the doorknob.

He hesitated at the door to his own apartment, across the hall from Kenzie's, because he heard someone crying. He leaned back, listening, and thought it was coming from Kenzie's apartment.

He finally went into his apartment, thinking it must be Wyatt, but not completely sure.

The next day the sign stayed on the door. Mrs. Costas had her meals brought to her room and told the waiter she had a little cold. Nodding decided not to bother her, despite his curiosity.

The following day he noticed the sign was no longer on her door, but he didn't want to miss a meeting with Toby and Hagan out at the barn. The Canada Day parade was coming up, and Hagan had called and asked to meet to discuss plans.

He refused to come into the lobby, and by the time Nodding got to the barn, Hagan and Toby had wheeled the float body outside. It seemed to be in fairly sound shape.

"The real reason I come over was to see exactly what you all were planning," Hagan said. "Nipper wants to make sure we don't screw up any of your ideas. A lot of people hear the HAGAN'S HAVEN name and think of this place."

"I haven't talked to Dave about it," Toby said, stepping back to survey the float body. "What I was thinking about was making a big blue star, like at the gazebo. Then we could have a rowboat aiming at it through the waves." He scratched his head and looked at Nodding. "I haven't come up with a good sign, but how about 'Steer for STILLWATERS' or 'Get Out of The Storm'?"

"Either would work," Nodding said. "People will recognize the star. Anyone walking on the beach at night can see it."

"I started out thinking of building a big cross to stand up, but Moses said it'd hit the electric lines. The star could be lower. I was prayin' hard the other night for an answer. When I opened my eyes and looked right up at the star. It just made sense."

"Well, Nipper likes the idea you gave him," Hagan said. "The money takes a little poke at the newspaper article and all, but it'll be fun."

"I haven't even heard about it," Nodding said.

"We're printing up fake dollars to hand out from the float. Anyone bringing in a Hagan dollar will get a free bag of chips with a purchase. Mixed in will be a few Nipper dollars, worth a dollar off a purchase. We have an ad coming out next week in the paper, saying 'HAGAN SHARE$ THE WEALTH.' Nipper even wants me and him and Jody to ride the float and throw out the dollars."

"Sounds like fun," Nodding said.

"Me and Nipper were wondering if your daughters would like to ride the float," Hagan said to Toby.

"Any sign of beer or liquor on the float?" Toby said.

"Against the town rules. Can't even hint at it."

"The kids might like it. I'll have to ask Jean."

"Think about it," Hagan said. "Nipper had the idea. He says parades are for kids, anyhow. We'd get a bunch of candy they could throw out."

"I think the whole idea sounds fum." Nodding said.

"It's gonna be. I went to the planning session last week. They have our floats near each other, and we follow a high school marching band. And I've been working on a surprise for that evening."

"Kitchen party?" Toby said.

"Even better on Canada Day," Hagan said. "We can't see fire-works anywhere near Port Medway. So we're having our own!"

"The guests will love it," Nodding said. "Where will they be?"

"I got clearance to shoot them from a barge just off the centre's beach," Hagan said. "Now this is something new, 'cause there won't be any loud bangs. Don't want to scare any wildlife or dogs. That part was Nipper's suggestion, and damned if the company I called doesn't have that as an option."

"Then Moses and I better get busy," Toby said. "I know he's ordered some paint and banners to cover the bare wood."

"Nipper wanted me to thank you guys for the fake money idea," Hagan said. "I guess I'll get going."

"Hold up," Toby said. "Dave didn't know about the floats, and this is the first I've heard about the fake dollars. Was it Moses gave you the idea?"

"I thought you all had talked about it," Hagan said. "That new desk clerk called over and talked with Nipper about it yesterday. He'd been thinking of having a few girls in bikinis on the float, just waving, but she convinced him the coupons would be more creat-ive."

"Mackenzie?" Toby looked at Nodding. "Didn't know she even knew about the parade, unless she heard something from Jean."

"No, not her. The older one. Nipper forgot her name."

"Wait," Nodding said. "Ask him when you go back. See if it was Mrs. Elliot."

"Her?" Hagan said. "The old lady with the pistol?"

"That woman is a true mystery," Toby said. "Do you think it could be her?"

"Shit," Hagan said. "This is gettin' good."

"If it's her, she's up to something," Nodding said. "She's a nice lady, but I don't know what's going on. Makes me nervous. How does she even know about Nipper and the parade?"

"I'll go ask Nipper what she said," Hagan said with a grin. "Just when things was starting to get dull."

"I'll talk with Moses," Toby said. "Maybe he knows something."

"I'll check with Virginia and Kenzie," Nodding said. "Let's keep in touch and see what comes up. The parade is only two weeks off, so we don't have a lot of time."

Nodding caught up with Virginia cleaning the office and asked Kenzie to come in from the desk. He explained the post cards, the newspaper interview, and the telephone call to Nipper.

"Jean told me all about the parking lot incident," Kenzie said. "Do you think that woman is really coming down here for the parade?"

"Sounds like she's here already," Virginia said. "Or else she's been reading the newspaper online, if she knows about the parade. But even then, the interview never mentioned parade floats." She stared at Nodding as though he'd missed something obvious.

"Well, keep your eyes open. She drives a big old Buick, so she'll be hard to miss. Let me know if she shows up. The guests wouldn't appreciate her pulling out a gun in the lobby."

"Speaking of old women, Mrs. Costas asked for you today," Kenzie said. "She said she had some suggestions for the manager."

"Great," Nodding said. "Has she come out of her room yet?"

"She's out," Virginia said. "Went out to the beach while we cleaned up. She was very pleasant to my girls."

"She said she's skipping lunch," Kenzie said. "But she wants her dinner brought up at seven."

"I guess I'll go up and say hello," Nodding said. "Let me know if Hagan calls the desk."

"She's still out in the gazebo," Virginia said. "Got a book out there with her, but I couldn't make out the title."

"She got all excited when I told her about the parade," Kenzie said. "She asked if we'd provide rides into Liverpool for guests who don't drive."

"I guess we'll have to," Nodding said. "Parking will be impossible." He left the office, stopping to say hello to an elderly couple in the lobby. They had just come from the chapel and were talking about the stained glass window.

"It's simply radiant," the man said. "This whole facility is wonderful."

Upstairs Nodding made a swing through the kitchen and found preparations beginning for dinner. He took a taste of the spaghetti sauce, nodded, and put the spoon on the tray to be washed. *Costas is what, a Greek name? She'll probably opt for the pot roast entree then. Costas.* The name was familiar.

Outside, he saw the woman in the gazebo, her back to him, reading. He started down the boardwalk, then stopped just short of the gazebo. Costas. What a fool he'd been.

"Costas was your husband's name," he told the woman's back.

"Afternoon, David." She put down the book and smiled as he came into the gazebo.

"I can't believe it," Nodding said. "Why the disguise, Mrs. Saks?"

Her lipstick clashed with the wig, but it worked. All you'd notice about her face would be the lipstick. "You had us going nuts this morning."

"Security around here doesn't exist," she said. "You can thank your lucky stars your guests are too religious to steal you blind.'

"There isn't much to steal," Nodding said. "Why are you here, by the way?" He went over and sat next to her on the bench.

"Why do you think, David?" She turned to face him, glancing around before she spoke. "Ever since January I've been living and breathing this terrorist business. It's all coming down to the line now, and I am ready for a break."

"You mean Wissam Mayoubi? The police think he's long gone.

He's not even from the middle east."

"He's not from near here," she said. "But don't you believe the stories you hear from the police. He's not long gone. He's heading our way and that's why I'm here."

"He's coming to Port Medway?" Nodding said. "He's on the run, Mrs. Saks. Why would he come here?"

"I'm reeling him in, David, and he doesn't know he's the bait for even bigger fish. That's all I can say for now, but I finally need your help."

"What can I do?" He knew it was easier to go along with her.

"Don't blow my cover. I'll keep a low profile and you go about your life as though nothing's wrong." She patted her wig carefully. "These things are simply dreadful and it isn't even hot yet."

"Is something wrong?"

"Not until Mayoubi gets to town," she said. "Then we have to be very watchful."

"Why would he come here?" Nodding asked again. "He's probably on the run and far from here, living it up."

"No, not with his problem. Is that black woman reliable? She has quick eyes."

"She's smart, and she's dependable. Back to Wissam. What's his problem?"

"All that money," Mrs. Saks said. "He never got it."

"Then who has it? The police said he snuck back and grabbed it."

"He didn't. Another mistake by the police. The problem is that Mayoubi thinks someone else has the money he wants. And he's looking very hard for it."

"Who has it?" Nodding said.

"That's a tough one. He thought you had it, until that interview slowed him down."

"Me?" Nodding said.

"You quit your job and left town," she said. "Mayoubi asked

around."

"And then he saw the interview."

"Now he's not sure. It may be that Hagan man. You're both in the same town now, so he ought to be along soon."

She stood up. "The breeze is shifting. I'd better get back inside."

"Are you feeling well?" Nodding got up to escort her.

"Fit as a fiddle," she said. "I take naps now and then, since I'm up most of the night."

"I'll keep everything quiet. But I can't have any guests hearing about Wissam and getting scared."

"They won't hear squat from me. I've let you in on it but no one else. You keep your eyes peeled, David, even if you still don't believe me."

They were just outside the dining room door. "It's nice to see you," Nodding said. "I keep some wine in my apartment, any time you feel like a visit."

"Oh, that kind I like? Don't tempt me, David." She winked. "You should offer a glass to that poor young girl who lives next to me. She needs it."

"Kenzie? Why?"

"She cried herself to sleep last night. Or if it was her little boy, she could still use the wine."

She stopped while Nodding opened the door for her. "Keep on your toes, dear."

And then she was off, moving quickly to the elevator, her book clenched in her crossed arms. He hadn't caught a glimpse of the title, either.

25: With bells on

Nodding went back toward his office, wondering what to do. Kenzie was at the desk, checking telephone charges. Most guests used their cell phones, but some still preferred the room phones.

He opened the office door and Virginia was there, dusting the filing cabinet.

"It's her, right?" She stopped dusting and looked at him.

"I'm not supposed to tell anyone," he said, coming in and closing the door.

"I've been here too long," Virginia said, waving her dust rag at him, "to fall for a crazy getup like that." She shook her head. "This here ain't no Oak Island or White Point. People don't come here for an adventure. They come here to find Jesus at the beach. Don't need a crazy wig for that."

"What do I do now?" There's an RCMP detective I know in Antigonish."

"If she's crazy all you'd do by calling a cop is cause a commotion. Let the old woman have her fun, as long as she doesn't upset the guests."

"What if she's not crazy?"

"Keep your eyes open, like she says." Virginia said. "I'll tell Moses, so the three of us can be watching things. She must have some kind of plan, or she wouldn't have set up that interview or pushed the parade idea."

"Sounds like she thinks he'll show up on Canada Day," Nodding said.

"Gotta clean the laundry room," Virginia said. "You're the boss, you figure it out."

She stopped by the door. "David, you got a gun somewhere?"

"No. Why would I?"

"Just in case, she has a little one in her bathroom, taped under the sink. Saw it when I delivered toilet paper."

"Thanks," he said, knowing he'd have to confront Mrs. Saks eventually.

Nodding spent part of the next afternoon helping Toby paint the float. The centre's truck would tow the wooden platform, and Moses had volunteered to drive. Kenzie said she'd stay behind to take care of the desk. Nodding would have to get back early to oversee dinner, so he agreed to help shuttle guests back and forth in the centre's van. Toby would take over after the parade, bringing back the last of the guests.

"Any word from the secret agent today?" Toby said. He was using a roller to apply a white base coat to the sides of the platform.

"Nothing," Nodding said. "Probably for the best. I don't know what she can find out from inside that apartment."

"You don't think she's right about this guy, do you?"

"I'd say no, except she had him figured out before. I don't think he's dangerous, anyway. But I've decided to alert the RCMP a few days before the parade, just in case."

"Better to be safe," Toby said. "Poor thing, probably doesn't want to go back to a quiet life."

"She has friends at home," Nodding said. "Says they're dull."

"Wish I could get her down for a hymn sing or something. Maybe I'll go up and invite her. I'd do that for any other guest. She don't have to know you filled me in. Give her a little Christian fellowship."

"Worth a try. What are you doing about a boat for this thing?"

"Moses has an old dory that won't float, but it'll work. He's painting it at home this week. How's Hagan's float coming along?"

"Want to go over this afternoon and check it out? You can meet Nipper and buy your lottery tickets."

"Long as we wait until after lunch. I have two elderly sisters sitting with me, discussing their favourite passages."

"Sounds like fun," Nodding said.

He shifted down a few feet to touch up a seam with his brush. The late morning sun felt good on his arms and neck, and he decided he should spend more time outside if work allowed.

After Nodding had served what seemed like a ton of tuna salad, the kitchen crew took over. He washed up and met Toby outside.

"I'll drive," Toby said, and they climbed into the red pickup.

"The last time I rode in this, we had an adventure," Nodding said.

"Still haven't replaced my Jesus," Toby said, looking at the statue on the dashboard. "Kinda like the way He sways around. I play my Amy Grant CD sometimes, and it looks like He's rocking to the music."

"I noticed you got one for the hotel van."

"Oh yeah, just a little one. There's a website where you can buy them. They got some that hold batteries. Their halos light up in the dark, so you can see them even at night."

"At least their eyes don't glow," Nodding said.

"That might be a bit tacky," Toby said. "Folks can overdo stuff like that, if they're not careful. First time Hagan rode with me, he just stared at my Jesus the whole time. Didn't say one word, which I figured was God's blessing. But the next day he gave me a ride, and darned if there wasn't an empty beer can glued to his dashboard."

"Did you say anything?"

"And give him the satisfaction? Heck no. Pretended I didn't notice a thing. It went away after a week or so."

He pulled up in front of Nipper's and parked the truck.

"Hey guys," Jody said. She was wearing a tight yellow HAGAN'S HAVEN tee shirt. "Watch this. I've been practising." She blew a fist-sized pink bubble and nodded.

"Dang," Toby said.

"Up," Jody said as the bubble popped. She scooped the gum into her mouth with a finger. "The guys are back in the office, unless you came in to see me."

"We better go back there," Nodding said. "Don't want to make them jealous."

"I don't know you," Jody said to Toby. "Radical truck you got there."

"Thanks," he said. "I'm Toby."

"Going to give me a ride sometime?" She snapped her gum and looked at him.

"Anytime," he said. "Bless you, now."

Nodding smiled at Jody's eyes, which seemed to slightly cross as she thought about Toby's comment. He led Toby back through the aisles.

"A ride with that girl would lead to temptation," Toby said. "Steer me straight on, Jesus."

"I think she could use a talk about spiritual life."

"We all could. But I'm not the one to deliver her sermon. No sir."

"My God, the Preacher," Hagan jumped up from his chair. He was holding a liquor catalogue, and Nipper was sitting at the desk. "You boys here for the beer special?"

"Came to talk about floats," Nodding said. "Nipper, this is Toby. He runs the program at the centre. Toby, this is Nipper Eisenhower."

"A pleasure to meet you, sir," Nipper said, reaching across the desk to shake hands. "Don't let this wild man get to you."

"God tests us all," Toby said. "He just gave me one out yonder."

"Hagan set us all up for that one," Nipper said. "He knew very well that shirt was too small when he gave it to her. Poor girl never thought to ask for a bigger one, either." He swung around and looked at a monitor, where Jody was blowing another bubble, and shook his head. "Mercy."

"We got our float almost ready, over at Nipper's house," Hagan said. "We fixed it so I can pull it with the tractor."

"We have a bench right after the HAGAN'S HAVEN sign," Nipper said. "I can sit up there and hand out coupons on one side. Jody will sit next to me and hand them out to the other side. We talked about it, and you folks can take the candy we got and hand it out. It's more proper for kids on your float."

"I told Nipper about your float with the dory," Hagan said. "Ours has to be pretty simple, or some old grump will complain we glorify drinking. But it will have red and white streamers and balloons to go with the flags. And we'll have Jody blowing bubbles."

"Anyone need some ammo?" Nipper opened his desk drawer and dropped a handful of chocolate kisses on the desk.

"I'd love to, but my wife warned me off sugar after Easter," Toby said. "She said it wasn't good for me."

"If I worried about what's good for people, I wouldn't be selling booze," Nipper said. "I gave up coffee this year for New Year's. One thing at a time." He unwrapped two kisses and popped them into his mouth.

"I have a little news," Nodding said. He told them about Mrs. Saks and her predictions.

"That pissant comes after me, I'll ship him home COD," Hagan said. "If *he* don't have the money, where'd it go?"

"As far as I know, he does have it," Nodding said. "But just in case, we ought to keep our eyes open."

"I'd stick a gun right up by the register, but Jody might shoot herself," Nipper said. "Besides, I don't have a gun. But I will turn on the outside camera."

"Nipper put it in when he had kids drinking by the loading dock," Hagan said. "Hasn't been a problem this spring."

"Damned kids would break all their bottles," Nipper said, reaching for another piece of candy. "Once the beer trucks started getting tire damage, I had to draw the line."

"Think it's safe for our kids to be near the floats?" Toby said. "What about Christine riding one?"

"At the moment I think it's safe," Nodding said. "But let's be sure the floats are right next to each other. That'll give us more people to keep an eye on things."

"I'll make sure of that," Hagan said. "But I won't say why. Don't want to make anyone nervous."

"I'll call Detective Martin next week," Nodding said. "But right now, I don't think it's worth getting upset."

"Nipper, you oughta come over to the centre and see what we've done to the place," Toby said.

"Come for dinner some evening," Nodding said.

"I just might, if someone could pick me up and bring me home," Nipper said. "I don't drive after dark anymore. But I should warn you, I'm not very devoted to organized religion. The last time I really talked to a minister was at my brother's funeral."

"I promise not to give you a sales pitch," Toby said. "I haven't even tried it on Dave. Not yet, anyhow."

"Give me a call," Nipper said. "I'll take you up on it. I can get a peek at your float, too."

"How about next Wednesday?" Toby said. "It's two days before the parade and the centre won't be packed mid-week."

He made a point of reaching across the desk to shake Nipper's hand, then followed Nodding out into the store.

"Nice man," Nodding said.

"Guys who own liquor stores are either nice folks or drunkards,"

Toby said. "Most of them deal with people who have problems, and they either handle it fine or they fall into the gutter." He waved a hand around at the shelves. "A few years ago I spent a lot of time in places like this. Bought all kinds of liquid friendship. Met some good people."

"You really a preacher?" Jody asked as they reached the counter.

"I'm really a truck driver," he said. "What are you?"

"Just plain old me," she said. "You come back and visit now."

"Like Daniel in the lion's den," Toby said. "Be good."

"Danny has a lion?"she said. "Guy up at the farm stand?"

Toby smiled and ducked through the door. "God loves all his creatures," he said to Nodding as they climbed into the truck. "But most women I know would not take kindly to Jody."

"You don't think she ought to come to dinner with Nipper?"

"That would be an adventure," Toby said. "But if the centre's guests didn't come after me for it, Jean might."

"As Nipper would say, 'Mercy,'" Nodding said.

"Amen. Can you whip up a good meal that don't have a lot of sugar for next week?"

"Fat's bad too. I'll make a good, healthy dinner we can all enjoy."

He sat back and began to plan a menu as they drove back. "Should we have Mrs. Saks stop in after we eat? I don't want her scaring Jean or the kids."

"I've already warned Jean about her," Toby said. "Let's see how things go."

The weekend went well. The hotel was full, and Mrs. Saks stayed in her apartment. Virginia reported to Nodding that she'd been warned to look for 'foreign tourist types', but she admitted she wouldn't know the difference.

In the few free moments he had, Nodding helped Moses and Toby work on the float. They built waves out of papier-mâché around the small dory Moses brought from home. They painted the waves blue and white, then lifted the star into place. Toby covered the star with sparkles, so that it would glimmer in the afternoon sun. They decided to make STILLWATERS signs to hang from the sides of the float, so there would be room for people in the dory.

On Tuesday Nodding called Nipper to confirm the dinner. Hagan's wife was making him go to a party at the golf club in Chester, so he couldn't attend. Nipper had an extra night clerk on the schedule, so he was free and excited about an evening away from the store.

Nodding set up the small, private dining room for the gathering. He invited Kenzie to join them, so Jean would feel more comfortable. He spoke with Moses, who said Virginia wouldn't attend because she didn't believe in "eating with the boss." Nodding pointed out they ate lunch together every day, but Moses said it didn't matter.

"Once Virginia makes up her mind, it's like concrete. The first thing I learned after we were married was how to surrender. It's the only way to keep peace over the years."

Nodding told Mrs. Saks he was having a guest over who was helping with the parade, and she agreed to come down for a little dessert.

"Is your guest Canadian?" she asked. "I already came to one little meeting and it turned ugly, don't you know."

"Yes he is," Nodding said. "He owns the local liquor store."

"I'll be there with bells on," she said. "Maybe he'll bring a bottle of that wine we like."

26: Don't you breathe a word

Nodding broiled chicken breasts, served them with fresh asparagus, and had a side salad with non-fat raspberry vinaigrette dressing. The popular choice in the main dining room was meatloaf with mashed potatoes and gravy, which Toby looked at hungrily before leaving to pick up Nipper. Jean had decided the girls and Wyatt could eat in the main dining room without their parents, as a treat.

"We early?" she said as she and Kenzie peeked in the door of the small dining room, tucked away beside the kitchen and away from the view.

"Come in," Nodding said. "They ought to be here soon."

"Toby said he doesn't walk too well?" Kenzie said.

"He has circulation problems because of his diabetes. He could probably control a lot of it through diet, but Hagan says he refuses and won't take his medication."

"Did we dress okay?" Jean looked worried and Nodding smiled. They were in long shorts with golf shirts, which was practically formal for the area. Kenzie saw him looking at them and smiled back.

"Made it!" Toby appeared as the elevator doors opened off the main dining room. "We're here and we're hungry."

The remaining hotel guests glanced up as Nipper limped across to the small room with his cane. He was wearing dark slacks, a sports shirt, and a new pair of fluffy slippers.

"It's Fred Flintstone," he said, waving a foot at Nodding. "And this one is Barney Rubble. Jody found them at Frenchy's. God only knows why they'd have them in adult sizes, but they're soft as feathers."

"God has His plan," Toby said.

"You promised," Jean said.

"Come in and we'll get started," Nodding said.

He seated the two men with the others, then nodded at the kitchen door. A waiter brought in their salads, while another brought in a basket of fresh brown bread, warm from the oven.

"Can we bow our heads for a moment?" Toby said, standing up. "Jesus, we thank you for the blessing of this meal we're about to share. We've travelled different roads to get here, and we thank you for the chance to enjoy our evening together. Amen."

"Russian?" Nipper said, holding up a piece of the bread.

"Authentic," Nodding said. "High in nutrition and flavour and easy to bake."

"Lucky Mrs. Saks isn't here quite yet," Toby said. "I bet she doesn't approve of foreign bread."

"My mother used to bake this bread," Nipper said. "Mercy, it's good to taste it again."

"Did you grow up here?" Kenzie asked. "I bet it was pretty and peaceful before tourists started to come."

"Some people think so," Nipper said. "But growing up here with dirt roads and old, toothless sailors wasn't my idea of beauty. I was bored to death."

"Why did you stay?" Jean asked.

"I left for a while," he said. "After I graduated from Dal I worked in Halifax. But when Dad passed away I came home and started the store with my brother."

He sniffed at the chicken the waiter put in front of him. "Dill? Mercy." He smiled.

"With some other herbs," Nodding said. "Just wrap the chicken and spices in foil and bake them. The chicken juices keep it moist."

"It smells heavenly," Nipper said, reaching for his knife.

"Tastes fine too," Toby said.

"I don't know how you do it," Kenzie said. "My husband yelled at me once for over-stuffing the turkey at Thanksgiving. It split in half and was all dry. After that he cooked for special occasions."

"Spices make the difference," Nipper said. "Even simple foods seem elegant."

"You know your cooking," Nodding said.

"I know eating. I used to cook a fair deal, when I was younger. Now I like a good meal every so often, but getting to the grocery is harder."

"Those weekly meal deliveries are worth looking at," Nodding said. "They send you the ingredients, and you can doctor them up to your preferences."

"I've been seeing the ads," Nipper said. "Maybe I'll give them a try."

As the waiters cleared the main-course plates, Nodding pulled an extra chair up to the table and announced there would be a guest for dinner.

"I hope I'm not too early?" Mrs. Saks stepped into the room, not wearing her wig or sunglasses.

"This is our mystery guest from the apartment upstairs," Nodding said. "Please welcome Mrs. Costas Sakalouckas, better known as Mrs. Saks."

"An honour, madam," Nipper said, partially rising in his chair.

"You must be the general," she said.

"Thank you for the title," Nipper said. "But I'm afraid I haven't earned it. Mr. Hagan has told me about your heroism this past winter, though."

"I could have been more effective with bullets," she said.

"Just confronting a thug takes courage," Nipper said. "Gun or no gun, trouble like that is frightening."

"David thinks I'm senile, but there's trouble heading this way."

"So I hear," Nipper said.

"Toby said something about it," Jean said. "Something about money?"

"As I understand it, a man named Wissam Mayoubi lost a lot of money," Nodding said. "Some pretty rough characters think it's their money, so he's trying to get it back before they catch up with him. And he apparently thinks Hagan and I have the money."

"That's what makes him dangerous," Mrs. Saks said. "That, and the fact that he's a terrorist."

The waiters appeared with a slice of cake for each of them.

"They'll come for the money during the parade," she said.

"Yummy. Angel food," Kenzie said. "Low in sugar."

Jean nodded, but she was looking carefully at Mrs. Saks. The conversation dwindled while they all enjoyed the dessert.

"We have a float ready to ride next to yours," Nipper said. "I think together we can keep an eye on everyone."

"I'll be there too," Mrs. Saks said. "And I imagine David will have called the police."

"How did you know?" he said.

"Because you have trust in these local folks. But their idea of excitement is a bad sunburn. We need military agents."

"How could you get them?" Nipper said, finishing his cake.

"You're the general," she said. "I'm just an old lady."

"The parade will be loaded with kids and families," Nodding said. "They won't risk anyone getting hurt."

"Those hooligans don't give a tinker's dam," Mrs. Saks said. "They eat their young, don't you know."

"Toby, is that true?" Jean said.

Toby winked at her.

"We'll be quietly prepared. It's how we do it in Nova Scotia," Nipper said. "Right, Mrs. Saks?"

"You bet your britches," she said, taking the last forkful of cake. "I have to scoot and check my email and cover my tracks. It's been an honour, General. Thank you all for inviting me."

"My pleasure, madam," Nipper said. He smiled as she peeked out at the dining room, then slipped away.

"Toby, I'm scared," Jean said. "This could be dangerous."

"Jesus is watching us, honey," he said. "We're dealing with a rug thief who's giving Mrs. Saks something to live for. All this talk of terrorists and missing money doesn't involve us. Have faith."

"No wonder Hagan is so excited," Nipper said. "This parade will be the highlight of the summer, unless I miss my bet. Do you think Mrs. Saks would consider riding on our float?"

"You can ask," Nodding said. "But I bet she'll prefer a lower profile. Besides, you want to save room for Jody."

"Mercy," Nipper said, smiling. "Now I better take my leave as well," he added, pulling himself up. "Thank you all for a delightful evening as well as a healthy and delicious dinner."

He grabbed his cane from the arm of his chair. "I promise not to eat any candy until tomorrow, at the earliest." He winked at Toby.

"That's the spirit," Toby said. "Was I that obvious?"

"I appreciate your concern," Nipper said. "I shall see you all on Friday, which they say will be a brilliant day."

He bowed at them and let Toby assist him to the elevator. "Thanks again, Davey," he called. "Goodnight, all"

"I hope you all know what you're doing," Jean said. "I'm worried about Christine on that float."

"I'll call the police tomorrow," Nodding said. "But if you want to keep her off the float, we'll understand."

"Well, I'll wait and see what the police say," she said. She turned to Kenzie. "You ready?"

"The kitchen crew is gone," Kenzie said. "I'll clear off the dessert dishes and pick up Wyatt in a few minutes." She looked at Nodding.

"Go ahead. Everything's done but the cake plates, he said. "But thanks."

"Thank you for inviting me," she said. "It was a delicious meal."

She and Jean left while Nodding took the dessert plates to the dishroom and rinsed them before turning out the lights.

When he got to his door he found a note from Mrs. Saks: "STOP IN. THE GAME IS AFOOT."

He knocked quietly and she answered through the door. "What's the password?"

"We don't have one."

"Just teasing, David." she said, opening the door. "You get so serious about all of this."

"Your note said something about the game?"

"Take a gander," she said, leading him over to the desk. A laptop was turned on, the cursor blinking patiently.

Mrs. Saks sat down and looked over her shoulder at Nodding. "Wissam Mayoubi, or whatever he calls himself, has been getting emails here for the longest time. I've been sending him notes now and then, trying to draw him out."

"How did you know his address?

"That day I followed him, remember he ate at the mall? He also went into a software store and checked his email. The dummy forgot to sign off, so I copied his email address."

"What messages did you give him?" Nodding said.

"I played lost and found. It doesn't take much to fool a terrorist, you know."

She tapped a few keys and brought up her mailbox.

"Why not go to the police and let them trace him?"

"It's useless if he's using a notebook. He could be anywhere. So I had to trick him to come out in the open."

"But you say guys are looking for him. You had to do it carefully."

"Now you're cooking with gas, David. He sent me a message

telling me a new email address for him. So then I sent a false clue to him on the old email, giving an address in Dartmouth. Two men broke in the very next day. So there really is someone after him."

"Why does he trust you?" Nodding asked.

"He thinks I'm as crooked as the Cabot Trail," she said. "I agreed to tell him where the money was, for a cut. I said my name was Ivanoff and I was working with the Russians."

"He agreed?"

"Sure, but he's planning to cheat me out of it, I know. Look here, this is the message asking which of you had the money. I sent him a notice about the interview so he could read it."

"What did you tell him about the money?" Nodding squinted at the screen.

"Said I didn't know. I said you were both simply scared to death. The money was hidden away, but it would be transferred to someone at the Canada Day parade because it was safe and public. He just had to come and snatch it and promise not to hurt anyone."

"So you plan to catch him trying to pick it up."

"That's the plan," she said. "Tonight I told him where the parade starts and to look for the HAGAN'S HAVEN float. The money would be there in a big briefcase."

"Why the parade?" he asked. "Why here and not in Antigonish?"

"You deserve to be in on it, David. Not at home, where I'd be all alone. The parade is the perfect place to catch a nasty man. Give him a taste of good old Canadian justice. Haul him off to the hoose-gow in front of hundreds of people waving Canadian flags."

"Can I let the police know?"

"Call the locals. But just to make you happy, I already faxed copies of my email chats to Detective Martin at home. By tomorrow morning he'll know what's going to happen."

"I have one question," Nodding said. "How do you know Hagan or I didn't steal that money? You could be telling the wrong people about your plan."

"Neither of you took it, plain and simple fact."

"You didn't see what we were doing."

"That's true," she said. "I was too busy taking the money myself."

She smiled as he took a step back. "It's under the bed in my suitcase, every stolen cent. It was almost too easy. You all went running off, so I opened the trunk of my little rental car, got out a rag to clean my gun, and dropped in the money."

"You should have given it to the police," he said. "If they find it now, you could be arrested."

"I haven't spent any. Though I ought to reimburse myself for that plane ride and this vacation. Besides, it's probably hooligan's drug money."

She wagged a finger at him. "Now, don't you breathe a word of this, David. It's going to be returned at the parade, just as promised."

"You're giving it to Mayoubi?"

"Just a little. The rest will be that fake money for the float."

She switched off the computer and stood up. "Once they have Mayoubi in handcuffs, I'll get rid of the briefcase once and for all."

"How much is there?" Nodding said, "The police think it's half a million."

"Close. Six hundred twenty thousand, in one hundred dollar bills. Now, you skedaddle and let me get my rest."

"Mrs. Saks—"

"Hush, now. It's too late to change anything without someone getting hurt. Let's just see what happens, David."

She pushed him gently out the door. "Goodnight, dear."

Standing in the hallway, staring at her door, Nodding realized he'd just become an accomplice. If he called the police now, and the money were discovered, the centre would be scandalized. He was helpless.

216

He turned toward his own door and noticed Kenzie peeking out of hers. She pulled it open when she saw him and waved him in.

"What's going on?" she whispered, shutting the door quietly. "I heard her talking to you."

"She's playing a dangerous game," Nodding said. "I hope it works out. I don't want her getting herself hurt or in trouble."

"I think she's cool," Kenzie said, her eyes bright. "Most people have such quiet lives when they get that old. Hers is more exciting than mine ever was."

"She may be imagining this whole thing," Nodding said. "Maybe there's no truth to it at all." He thought about the suitcase of money and the gun taped under the sink and decided to keep quiet.

"I made some coffee," she said. "Want a cup?"

"I'd love one. Black is fine." He noticed the larger bedroom shared a wall with Mrs. Saks. The door was closed now, so they wouldn't have a listener if they stayed in the main room.

"Things working out so far?" he said, taking the mug she handed him. It was steaming, so he decided to let it cool for a minute.

"I love it here," she said. "Why?"

"Sometimes you don't look happy," he said, blowing at the coffee.

"Oh, I'm nervous about the future. I don't know how long this job will last, and I worry about how I can take care of Wyatt." She sipped her own mug. "I didn't know it was obvious. I'm sorry."

"There's nothing to be sorry for. I just wondered if there was anything I could do to help."

The coffee was cooler and he took a sip. "I'm worried, too. I don't know what I'll do if this doesn't work out. But I needed a change, so here I am."

"Tell me about it," she said with a smile. "If it weren't for you guys, I don't know what I'd be doing in Halifax. I was falling apart." She blinked and reached for her mug.

"Toby and Jean are pretty good people," he said.

"Jean's an angel. When my marriage was falling apart, I really thought it was my fault. But she stood up for me and supported me the whole way."

"You got separated last fall?"

"Didn't really separate. He just left." She shook her head. "I guess everyone changes. We just grew apart, except I didn't realize it."

She looked up. "I'm sorry, I shouldn't be talking about this."

"Why not? None of us were really happy before, or we wouldn't be here now."

"I hadn't thought of it that way," Kenzie said. She took a deep breath. "When Rick and I first got together, we had a great time. We went away on weekends, we partied, and we had a pretty wild life. But that was before Wyatt came along."

"Kids change things," he said.

"Wyatt did for me. Rick made me quit working to stay home and then wanted us to keep living like we used to. I just couldn't do it." She shook her head. "I guess it was then he started seeing other women, but I didn't suspect anything."

"Did he fall in love with someone else?"

"No, that's just it. He just got tired of me. He said I was too dull. And that really hurt me."

She looked down at her cup. "It got to be where the only time we spent together was having sex, and finally he said I was boring then."

Her face was flushed, and there were tears on her cheeks. "I'm sorry, I shouldn't have said that."

"He sounds pretty lonely to me," Nodding said. "He didn't deserve you." He put down his mug. "I better go, but thanks, Kenzie."

He opened the door and looked back. "You are not boring. Goodnight."

Slipping into his own door, he wondered if he'd made a fool of himself.

27: Goodness

The next morning at ten-fifteen, Detective Martin called from Antigonish. "You know anything about this fax I got? Looks like the old woman has hit pay dirt."

"She's staying here at the centre," Nodding said. "She told me she was sending you the information. The money she intends to give Mayoubi is mostly fake bills printed up for the parade."

"Could get dangerous if anyone figures out it's a trick."

"You met the lady. She contacted you because she knows it could be dangerous. She's a little eccentric."

"And the Pope's a little Catholic," Martin said. "Gotta tell you, she's pissed me off. Now I have to come over and get involved in all this. Plus, I gotta work with the local RCMP, who may not fall in love with me being there. The whole situation sucks, the way she's set it up."

"Tell me about it," Nodding said. "I'm stuck right in the middle. The guy thinks Hagan and I used his money to move here and get into the hotel business."

"Yeah, maybe. Didn't take much to verify the lottery story. Could be Mayoubi did the same thing and won't show."

"I hope he doesn't."

"If I gotta tell my wife I'm going to the Atlantic Ocean and leaving her home on Canada Day, he damned well better show."

"Bring her along. We always keep a room open for emergencies. The two of you can stay over, on the house, if you don't mind being at a religious conference centre."

"You serious?" Martin said. "I might just take you up on that, Nodding. My wife and I are pretty regular church people. I could drop her off and then meet with the local troops before the parade starts. You really mean it?"

"I feel guilty getting you dragged down here," Nodding said. "Yes, the room will be ready anytime after dinner this evening."

"I appreciate it. We'll keep a low profile around your floats, but don't worry. If he shows, he's history."

Nodding hung up, took a deep breath, and smiled. Things might work out.

Then he got involved in centre business again until late in the afternoon. He called Hagan, talked with Toby, and sent a message to Mrs. Saks, who wasn't answering her telephone.

Canada Day was bright and almost hot, as Nipper had promised. Moses drove the float into Liverpool at ten, even though the parade didn't start until noon. Floats lined up near the playground, and before long Hagan arrived on Nipper's tractor, towing the HAGAN'S HAVEN float.

"Where's the suitcase?" Nipper said. He was sitting on the float's bench, wearing red pants and a white shirt. He had on his Fred and Barney slippers. "Mrs. Saks said she had a suitcase for us to use with our Hagan dollar coupons."

"Have to ask Dave," Moses said. "He and Toby are due with the van."

"Mercy," Nipper said, pointing down the street.

Jody was climbing out of a Jeep. She waved at the boy driving it and started their way. She was wearing a skin-tight red spandex bodysuit with a white maple leaf on her chest. She had topped it off with a white baseball cap and white sneakers.

"Like my costume? I was going to chew bright red gum and all, but it kinda looked like blood. So pink will have to do."

"Lordy, I think I'll look for Mrs. Saks," Toby said.

He and Nodding had just arrived, but he moved off into the growing crowd.

"Last year I was out on the beach and fell asleep," Jody said. "I missed the parade and got sunburned so bad I couldn't stay awake for the Liverpool fireworks."

"We may have earlier fireworks today," Nipper said.

"Far out," Jody said. "I just love the big ones. They scare me."

"Time to climb up on the bench and keep Ike company," Hagan said. He went to check the back of the float.

Nodding had wandered through the crowd for a while, then came back as the bands began to warm up. "I think it's a false alarm," he said. "It's pretty quiet."

Christine arrived with Jean, who said she was still nervous. "I couldn't stand not being here," she said. "Do you think it's safe?"

"We're all right here," Toby said. "Look to Jesus and he'll calm you."

He helped Christine onto the centre's float, while Jody brought over two buckets of candy for her to throw. She sat in the front of the float, and Toby climbed into the dory. He pulled on a yellow rain jacket and hat.

"I'm likely to sweat enough to float this here boat," he said. "But I can stay close to Christine this way."

"I have my window open," Moses said. "Just shout if you need me."

He climbed into the pickup and started the engine.

Nodding walked over to the other float as Hagan climbed into the tractor seat.

"Where's the old woman?" Hagan said. "Ain't like her to miss the parade, is it?"

"No, and I'm worried. There's no suitcase, either."

"Oh, it's here," Jody said. "I put it in the carton with the Nipper

221

dollars. I covered them with a blanket from the bench so they wouldn't blow away."

"Shit," Hagan said, swinging around. "You need them where you can reach them, Jody. You have to throw them off the float, remember?"

"Oh yeah," Jody said. "I forgot that part."

"We're moving," Toby yelled. Hagan gunned the tractor and the float lurched forward. Jody knelt and pulled a suitcase out from a box under a blanket. She slid it forward on the floor, then took a handful of printed Hagan dollars out of the box and stood up.

Nodding walked behind Hagan's float as it pulled out into the road, where he caught sight of Mrs. Saks at the curb. She was scanning the crowd, but ducked back out of sight before he could get her attention.

"We're rolling, Jesus," Toby said. "Keep your eye on us now, and please keep us safe."

The band started to play and Toby stopped yelling.

The parade halted after a block, and Nodding watched Christine throw a handful of candy to a group of children. He turned to watch Jody throw a wad of the fake dollars to applauding adults. A group of children were with them, yelling for candy, so Jody pointed to the STILLWATERS float. With them was a man in a long white robe, who said something to Jody.

"Dude, you look like that guy in the Bible," she said.

"You mean him?" Nipper swung around to see the robed man. "Looks like when Charleston Heston played Moses."

"What?" The front of the float veered to the left as Moses stuck his head out to hear.

"It's him," Toby yelled, pointing at the man.

"Who?" Moses yelled, straightening out the float.

Mayoubi leapt at Hagan's float, his eyes on the suitcase at Jody's feet. "It is mine," he said. He pulled a knife out of his robe and waved it over his head.

"Dude," Jody yelled, throwing a wad of coupons at his face.

Mayoubi staggered backwards a step. He hesitated a moment, and then two men were behind him, dragging him off the float and toward the curb. Nodding saw handcuffs flashing, and recognized Martin as one of the men.

"Yes," Nipper shouted, throwing a handful of coupons into the street. "God bless the Mounties!"

"I am a taxpayer," Wissam shouted, struggling with the policemen.

Nodding saw Toby, who had started to get up, settle back into the dory and smile.

At the curb, Mrs. Saks appeared.

"Dear woman, why is it always you?" Wissam looked up at her as he was being frisked.

"I knew you'd take the bait," she said, wagging a finger at him. "You couldn't resist the lure of the crowd. Besides, a true Canadian would never steal on Canada Day."

"I came for my money. I have to pay the others or they will kill me."

"Rotten to the core," Mrs. Saks said. She glared as he was led away.

Nodding turned as the parade started to move again, and saw two men in sunglasses walking toward the floats, on the other side of the street from Wissam and Mrs. Saks.

One of the men jumped up beside Hagan on the tractor and held a pistol to his head. The other jumped onto the float and made a grab for the suitcase.

Nodding didn't have time to think. As the tractor gunned its engine, he stepped to the first float and grabbed Christine by her dress. He carried her to the curb, and saw Mrs. Saks pointing at the float.

"Moses," Toby was up in the boat, holding its sides for balance.

"What?" Moses said, sticking his head out again.

"Yo! Get off." Jody grabbed another handful of coupons and threw them at the man in the float. He reached for the suitcase but fell to his knees as the float swerved.

Jody lost her balance and staggered, bumping into the man. He grabbed her and stood up, using her as a shield while he reached for the suitcase.

Moses veered, hoping to cut off the tractor, but the man next to Hagan fired two shots into the pickup, shattering the rear window.

The truck swung to the right and slowed, and the tractor began to pull around the float.

"Get down," Toby yelled, but people were already diving for the sidewalk, pulling their children back to safety.

Nodding saw Martin waving his badge, pushing through the crowd. He turned back to the floats in time to see Nipper dive off the bench and tackle Jody, ripping her away from the man who had just grabbed the suitcase and then lost it.

The suitcase dropped off the float into the street, and the man jumped after it. He landed in front of two policemen with drawn pistols.

The tractor swung past the rear of the centre's float, and Nodding saw Toby, his yellow hat crooked, standing in the dory and holding an oar. The man standing next to Hagan was looking at his partner being arrested.

"Jesus," Toby said, and the man turned.

There was a smack as the oar hit the man in his face, knocking him off the tractor and into the street.

"Amen," Toby said. "I smote that sinner."

Nodding turned to see Martin and other officers surrounding the fallen man, who appeared to be groggy but conscious.

"Yeah, Daddy!" Christine stepped out from behind Nodding.

The floats stopped, and the people on the street suddenly began to applaud. Toby, with his yellow hat sideways on his head, smiled sheepishly and climbed down.

Moses was climbing out of the pickup, brushing a bit of glass from his hair and looking scared. "Any more of this nonsense and I'm moving," he said. "This here doesn't happen in Nova Scotia."

"Dude!" Jody said, climbing to her feet. She helped Nipper stand up and limp back to the float bench, and then gave him a kiss.

"Mercy," he said, blushing. The crowd cheered again.

"You could have been killed, but you risked your life for me," Jody said. She looked up as Nodding climbed onto the float. "This is one manly dude," she said. "But I gotta pee." She disappeared around the corner of the float.

"Nice move," Nodding said. "Are you okay?"

"I didn't know you could jump that fast," Hagan said, coming up beside them. "That damned pissant with the gun scared the shit out of me."

"He was grabbing her chest," Nipper said. "Just not proper." He glanced at Jody as she made her way through the crowd along the edge of the road.

"You manly dude," Hagan said. "What were you grabbing?"

"Mercy," Nipper said.

He glanced around, then dug into his pants. "I had a frozen candy bar in my pocket, is all. But I believe it got smashed."

"Shit," said Hagan. "This beats everything."

Nodding looked down at the man lying in the street, moaning now. Toby was on his knees beside him, praying.

"Nodding," Detective Martin said. "These fools followed Mayoubi all the way here and almost got away with a suitcase full of liquor store coupons. The old lady set it up perfectly." An ambulance was working its way up the street for the injured man, and Jean was there, hugging Christine and crying.

"I don't see Mrs. Saks," Nodding said. "She was right here."

"She's a weird one," Martin said. "But it's been worth the trip, I'll tell you. Got Mayoubi and these two lowlifes, all because she tricked them."

Nodding wandered over to the curb, where two uniformed policemen were standing with Mayoubi.

"David, it's good to see you, my friend." Mayoubi nodded, but he didn't smile. "I wish we were in another place, though."

"You should have kept going, Wissam."

"It was my money. I stole a truck to earn it, so I had to get it back. That woman from hell destroyed me twice."

"Look there," one of the policemen said, pointing up.

A single engine plane was making a low pass over the parade, towing a banner that said OH CANADA!

"Pilot has his numbers covered up," the policeman said. "Kinda strange."

"Dave, how can we thank you?" Jean said as she came up to him, holding Christine's hand and still crying. "You saved my baby."

"She would have jumped off anyway," Nodding said. "Right, Christine?"

"Yeah," Christine said. "I spilled the candy, Mom."

"We owe you, Dave," Toby said, coming up to shake his hand. "Jesus was with us today."

"You're the hero of the day," Nodding said. "Looks like it all worked out, other than the parade ending after one block."

"Now he's really low," the policeman said, pointing. "He's not allowed to do a low flyover."

Nodding looked up as the airplane came back, less than two hundred feet off the ground.

Just as it got close, something dropped out of the door, then came apart as it fell, becoming a shower of bills as the breeze caught it.

The crowd began to scream as the money reached the parade route.

The plane circled back before flying away, allowing a passenger to look out. Nodding was probably the only one who saw the smiling face and the waving hand.

He waved back at Virginia.

28: Why are you laughing?

Martin had briefed the local police and RCMP officers from sur-rounding towns, so the questions were few. The crowd dwindled quickly once money stopped falling, and children ran home with hundred dollar bills instead of parade candy. Hagan and Nipper swore they had no idea who dropped the money, even though some Hagan coupons were mixed in.

"No money's been reported stolen, so there's no crime involving the RCMP," Martin said. "I can't prove this money is involved with the truck theft, so it's over."

As he went off to the station to do paperwork, he waved at Nod-ding. "Tell my wife I'll be along soon."

Nipper and Hagan found Nodding before everyone left. "I'm tak-ing us out to dinner," Nipper said. "This has been more excitement than I've had in awhile. Want to join us?"

"I'd love to, but I can't. We have a hotel full of guests, and Toby has a chapel program before the fireworks, Besides, I want to see if Mrs. Saks is there."

"She's not," Nipper said. "Mercy, what excitement. She called me yesterday and I arranged that little airplane stunt with a friend of mine. But she planned to leave from the parade for a trip, just in case."

"Where's she going?"

"She said Cuba, but it may be a cover story. She'll be back once things calm down."

"How do you know?" Nodding said.

"I hired her," Nipper said. "Put her in charge of security for the store. Told her you could use some security, too, so she may come calling."

"Do you need any security?"

"Not that I know of, but we'll think of something for her to do. It's too much fun to stop now, Davey."

Hagan gunned the tractor, and Nipper waved goodbye.

Nodding, in the van with a small load of guests, followed Toby and the float back to Port Medway. When they pulled into the lot, Jean, Kenzie, the kids, and a few of the guests were there to cheer.

"The Lord has guided us into a safe harbour," Toby said, climbing out of his truck. "We're safe on the shores."

"You weren't in a real boat," Christine said. "It's only a float, Dad."

"He just means we're all safe at home, sweetie," Jean said.

"I was so worried," Kenzie said. "They said on the radio someone had been hurt and there were gunshots."

Nodding turned, smiling, and she was looking at him. Toby and Jean had turned away. "I'm so glad you're safe." She began blinking and Nodding put his hands on her shoulders.

"Everything's over," he said. "We're okay." Then she was hugging him, and he saw Toby look over and smile.

"I'm sorry," she said, pulling back. "I had no right to do that. I'm sorry." She turned and hurried toward the lobby. Jean and the kids followed her.

Nodding went over to where Toby was unhooking the float from his truck. "What was that about?" he said. "Did I miss something?"

"You've been missing it, Dave," Toby said, putting his hand on Nodding's shoulder. "The signs have been there for a couple of weeks, but you've had your blinders on." He smiled. "Guess it's up to you now. The dear Lord done His part."

Nodding walked into the lobby and went straight to the office. He wasn't surprised to find Virginia waiting for him.

"I knew I was dumb to wave," she said. "I pulled off that big trick and then waved at you there, standing next to the police."

"They didn't see you," Nodding said. "Too busy chasing the money. Where was the plane from?"

"Don't even ask. It's long gone now. Nipper has friends from away."

"Looked like a lot of money floating down," he said.

"Mrs. Saks said not to tell the pilot, else he might take it and throw *me* out. So I didn't count it."

"For that much money he might have."

"He got paid well," she said. "Twenty thousand, cash."

"I hope she paid *you* well for taking that risk."

"I'm happy," Virginia said.

"Gonna retire?"

"What would I do retired?" she said. "I'd be bored just sitting at home, and I can only clean it so much. So I'll be here in the morning. I just stopped by to say thanks for not saying it was me up there."

"How do you know I didn't?" Nodding smiled at her.

"I'd be in jail already," Virginia said. "And you'd be making beds yourself tomorrow morning."

At the door she turned and smiled. "Think I'll take Moses out tonight," she said. "Poor man needs a little treat."

Nodding went up to the kitchen to help with dinner. He stayed through the meal, grabbing a bite to sustain himself, then went down and took over the desk. Finally, when most of the guests had gone out to wait for the fireworks, he climbed up the steps to his apartment.

Mrs. Saks had left her door open and the apartment clean. Her computer was still there, but taped to the screen was a note: "I'LL

BE BACK FOR THIS!"

Nodding smiled at the screen and went to his apartment. From his living room he could see the boardwalk, gazebo and the beach, all crowded with guests and nearby residents. He went across the hall and knocked on Kenzie's door to invite them over to watch the show.

He went back to his living room and opened the window. Wyatt hurried in, already in his pajamas. Nodding got him a glass of apple juice and poured a glass of wine for Kenzie.

"I'm really sorry," she said, while they watched Wyatt waiting for the show to begin. "I shouldn't have let myself get upset. I embarrassed you in front of everyone."

"I'm only embarrassed because I've been so out of it," he said. "You didn't do anything to be sorry for."

"I'll understand if you want me to leave," she said. "What? Why are you laughing?"

"Because that's something I'd say. I don't want you to leave. I'm just getting to know you."

"You probably know about all there is," Kenzie said. "I'm dull."

"You're not dull, Mommy," Wyatt said. He turned back as Toby turned off the outside lights and the fireworks began.

"Wyatt's right," Nodding said.

"Christine said everyone is special," Wyatt said, still watching the sky.

They stood behind Wyatt and watched the flashes, not missing the loud explosions. Kenzie said she liked the bright red rockets best, but Nodding preferred the gold. Wyatt said they were all his favourites.

In twenty minutes the show was over, leaving the sky empty except for a fading cloud of smoke.

"I better get him to bed," Kenzie said.

"Thanks," Wyatt said. "You can come to church with me sometime."

"Wyatt," Kenzie said, looking at Nodding.

"You can come back if you want," he said. "We could talk."

"I guess I could hear him if I left the door open," she said, putting down her wine glass. "But why don't you come over instead? I'll let you know when he's asleep. You can bring me another glass of wine."

When Kenzie and Wyatt were in their apartment, Nodding sat down by the open window. To his left he could see the Port Med-way light, but straight out the window it was dark. He could hear the waves lapping on the beach. He looked down, trying to see the water.

Below him he saw Toby, lying next to the empty gazebo, looking up at his neon star, which was casting a blue mist in the moist night air.

Nodding leaned out and looked down at Toby, who rolled over and sat up. Their eyes met briefly and Toby waved. Nodding smiled as he pulled back into his room.

He took a deep breath and, for a moment, closed his eyes.

"Amen," he said. He opened his eyes and looked out at the dark water. Below him, Toby swung around to face out, and they both sat watching the sea.

James O. Weeks

Acknowledgements

A life filled with fascinating individuals has inspired my efforts, but four writers taught and shaped my ability. Max Steele, John Gardner, and George Friedman informed and supported my efforts. Andrew Wetmore at Moose House took a chance and allowed this novel to be shared. I will be forever grateful to them.

A group of fellow writers who meet monthly to share and support has given me wise advice on my writing, for which I thank them.

James O. Weeks

About the author

James O. Weeks taught English in secondary schools and community college for forty years. He published articles in professional journals and short genre fiction (*Wilderness Tales*) while teaching young adults about writing. His work appears in Moose House's second collection of short fiction, *Blink and You'll Miss It*.

Beyond the classroom, Jim worked as a swimming pool manager, camp counsellor, and liquor store clerk, and for twelve years was a driver and pump operator for a volunteer fire department.

Jim and his wife (a fifth-generation Nova Scotian) live in Lunenburg.

Nodding's People is his first novel.